'Ah, Gina,' Mrs Knebworth said, lowering her newspaper as Gina came into the room.

'I'm just heading out to the Modern Art Gallery to meet Dermot for an hour or so, remember? You said that would be OK.'

'Oh dear, Gina . . .' Mrs Knebworth shook her head.

'What?'

'Dating is delightful, but breaking up is never easy. Good luck.'

Gina's mouth fell open with surprise. Everybody knew. Every single person knew. This was a nightmare! What if she got to the gallery and suddenly felt just as crazy about Dermot as she had when they'd first started going out? Then everyone would keep asking why she hadn't dumped him.

And what if he got to hear about her plan?

What if he already knew?

Also available by Carmen Reid:

Secrets at St Jude's: New Girl
Secrets at St Jude's: Jealous Girl
Secrets at St Jude's: Drama Girl
Secrets at St Jude's: Rebel Girl

For adult readers:
The Personal Shopper
Did the Earth Move?
Three in a Bed
Up all Night
How Was it For You?
Late Night Shopping
How Not To Shop
Celebrity Shopper
New York Valentine

www.carmenreid.co.uk
www.secretsatstjudes.co.uk

Secrets at St Jude's

SUNSHINE GIRL

Carmen Reid

CORGI BOOKS

SECRETS AT ST JUDE'S: SUNSHINE GIRL
A CORGI BOOK 978 0 552 56368 0

First published in Great Britain by Corgi Books,
an imprint of Random House Children's Books,
A Random House Group Company

This edition published 2011

1 3 5 7 9 10 8 6 4 2

The Random House Group Limited supports The Forest Stewardship
Council (FSC), the leading international forest certification organisation.
All our titles that are printed on Greenpeace approved FSC certified paper
carry the FSC logo. Our paper procurement policy can be found
at www.**randomhouse**.co.uk/environment

Mixed Sources
Product group from well-managed
forests and other controlled sources
www.fsc.org Cert no. TT-COC-002139
© 1996 Forest Stewardship Council

Set in 12/16pt Minion
Corgi Books are published by Random House Children's Books,
61–63 Uxbridge Road, London W5 5SA

www.**kidsatrandomhouse**.co.uk
www.**totallyrandombooks**.co.uk

Addresses for companies within The Random House Group Limited
can be found at: www.**randomhouse**.co.uk/offices.htm

THE RANDOM HOUSE GROUP Limited Reg. No. 954009

A CIP catalogue record for this book is available from the British Library.

Printed and bound in Great Britain by
CPI Bookmarque, Croydon, CR0 4TD

MEET THE ST JUDE'S GIRLS ...
GINA

Full name: Gina Louise Winkelmann-Peterson

Home: A fabulous white and glass architect-designed beach house with pool on the Californian coast

Likes: Sunshine (sadly not often found in Edinburgh), swimming, Halloween, pointy ankle boots, Prada or anything Prada-esque, Reece's Pieces, her cell phone, her little brother Menzie (sometimes), coffee, Dermot O'Hagan ... and Callum Cormack

Dislikes: Slithery octopus-type kisses, the totally gross sludge-green St Jude's school uniform, deadly dull history lessons, Charlie Fotherington-whatsit, boiled vegetables of any kind (I mean guys, like haven't you heard of stir-fry?)

Would like to be: A sreenwriter – but absolutely no one in the whole world knows about that

Fascinating fact: Gina has three other best friends at her old school in California – Paula, Ria and Maddison. They still can't believe she goes to boarding school in Scotland

NIFFY

Full name: Luella Edith Millicent Pethurer Nairn-Bassett (no wonder she's called either 'Niffy' or 'Lou')

Home: The ancient, crumbling, ancestral mansion Blacklough Hall in Cumbria, England

Likes: Playing pranks, enormous horses and slobbery dogs, all team games (especially hockey – she's really good), the St J's assembly game Banshee Buzzword Bingo (which she invented), her big brother Finn, the odd sneaked glass of expensive red wine, all school food, but especially pudding

Dislikes: Dresses, dressing up, poncy shoes and fussy clothes of any description, make-up, fussing with her hair, fussing about anything at all, her real name

Would like to be: A professional rider – an international show-jumper, or maybe a three-day eventer – that way she could do show jumping, dressage and her favourite, cross-country jumping

Fascinating fact: She can be fully dressed in all her riding clothes and hat in twenty-five seconds flat

MIN

Full name: Asimina Singupta

Home: A big family house with a huge garden in a suburb of Durban, South Africa

Likes: Running really, really fast and winning, being top of the class in every single subject, doing homework (it's so interesting when you really get into it), mango lassis, gold bracelets, reading science books, borrowing Amy's clothes, her mum's home-made curries

Dislikes: The sight of blood, biology lessons, babysitting her little brothers and sisters, the food at St J's, wearing her hair in plaits, Scottish grey skies

Would like to be: A medical researcher or medical physicist. She has to do something medical because of her doctor parents but it can't involve blood!

Fascinating fact: Min's mother taught herself Italian and went all the way to Pisa to get her medical degree

AMY

Full name: Amy Margaret McCorquodale

Home: Recently forced to downsize from an amazing penthouse flat in Glasgow, Scotland, with a terrace and panoramic view of the city

Likes: Designer jeans (Iceberg), designer bags (Marc Jacobs), designer boots (Jimmy Choo, but only when her dad is feeling incredibly generous), Edinburgh's Harvey Nichols (obviously), very handsome boys, diamonds, champagne, dance music, dressing up and going out, her gran's mince and tatties

Dislikes: Penny Boswell-Hackett, Mrs Norah 'the Neb' Knebworth, everything in Niffy's wardrobe, French lessons, people teasing her about her Glaswegian accent, oh and Penny Boswell-Hackett (have you got that?)

Would like to be: Officially, she's going to do a law degree, then join her dad's nightclub business. Secretly, she'd like to be a famous and fabulous actress

Fascinating fact: Amy's mum and dad were teenagers when she . . . er . . . arrived. She was brought up by her dad, her gran and her grandpa. She hasn't seen her real mum for years

Chapter One

'When does this film finish?' Gina hissed against the ear of the very handsome boy sitting next to her.

'I don't know,' he whispered back right against her ear, sending a little shiver down her neck.

'But I have to be somewhere else by four!'

'*Shhh*!' Again, he leaned across the small space which separated them and kissed her right on the mouth.

Gina closed her eyes and forgot all about the film they were supposed to be watching, and the other place she was supposed to be in twenty minutes. She kissed him back. Kissed and kissed. No one that she'd ever kissed before kissed quite the way that Callum did.

When his kisses started, she didn't want them to stop. In fact she wanted them to go further and deeper, she wanted to wrap her arms around him and let him kiss, kiss, kiss her for ever.

But all of a sudden, the kiss stopped abruptly and he

let her go. He glanced briefly at the screen, then slipped off his leather jacket and pulled his T-shirt right up over his head and off! Now he was sitting bare-chested in his seat.

Gina looked at him, mouth open with astonishment. 'What are you doing?'

'Trying to give you ideas,' he replied.

This made her giggle and she couldn't help herself from taking a good look at the parts he'd just revealed. His chest was smooth, with solid-looking pecs, and now she was checking out his narrow waist and the fuzzy skin just beneath his tummy button.

'I'm not taking my top off in the cinema,' she whispered.

He leaned over again. He was going to kiss her, and she was almost dizzy at the thought of feeling his bare skin pressed right up against her.

'Go on,' he urged, his lips just about touching hers. 'It's pitch-black, no one else will see. We'll just sit here without any clothes on until the credits run and then we'll get dressed again. Think how much fun we'll have. And no one will know a thing.'

Gina pointed her finger and tapped it against her head to let him know that he was completely nuts.

He reached down and began to take off his shoes and

then his socks. The cinema wasn't exactly full, because it was a sunny Saturday afternoon, but the handful of other people in their row were now turning their heads to look.

'Callum!' Gina protested, as he began to make a start on the waistband button of his jeans. 'You'll get us thrown out. You might even get arrested.'

Callum just smiled. 'C'mon,' he said, reaching for the place where her top met her skirt. 'Dare you to sit in the cinema in your underwear.'

'No!' she squeaked, hearing the buzz of his jeans zipper being undone despite the loud bangs, gunfire and screams coming from the film.

But this, Gina was learning, was the thrill of being out with Callum. Anything could happen. Anything *did* happen!

Now he was shuffling about in his chair, trying to pull down his jeans.

Gina part wanted to stop him, part couldn't bear to tear her eyes away. Was he really, really going to do this? Sit in the audience in his smalls?! Was he going to get away with this? Her eyes scanned the room to see if anyone was marching down the aisle to tell him off yet.

What kind of underwear would he have on? She suddenly had a burning urge to know.

Still she managed to whisper to him: 'Callum, put your clothes on!' But then she was caught in a bare-chested kiss once again and so wound up by it she was almost forgetting to breathe.

'Shall I take my jeans off?' he whispered against her ear. 'Do you dare me? Would you still kiss a guy who was only wearing boxers? Would you risk it?'

Music had struck up. Gina opened her eyes and saw that the film was over.

'Credits . . .' she warned him. 'Any moment now and—'

It had already happened.

'Lights,' she pointed out with a smile.

'Uh-oh . . .' Callum zipped up the jeans, but sat back in his seat, bare-chested and smiling happily, as other cinema-goers began to stand up and walk out of the row, stepping over his shoes and socks as they did so. 'Hi . . . hello there . . . hot in here today, isn't it?' he asked one passing girl.

This was making Gina laugh. He was completely outrageous: an ever-smiling, cheeky, naughty boy. She could not get enough of him.

'Where are we going next?' he asked, a grin breaking out across his face.

Gina took a look at her slim wristwatch – a present

from her mom when Gina was about to leave California and travel all the way to Edinburgh, Scotland, to become a boarder at St Jude's School for Girls.

'Oh! It's five to four already!' she exclaimed. 'I have to go! I'm going to be late. And you know you can't come with me.'

'Is *he* going to be there?' Callum asked, big emphasis on the 'he'.

'Yes, he is definitely going to be there.'

'What I want to know, Gina,' Callum began, throwing his bare arm round her shoulders, 'is just exactly when is *he* going to be out of the picture? Because I want to have you all to myself.'

Chapter Two

'Are you sure it's OK for us to be here today?' Amy flicked her long blonde hair from her face and shot Dermot a smile. 'I mean, not that long ago we got thrown out of here and your dad told us never, ever to come back again.'

Dermot, a very friendly looking guy with sandy-brown hair, blue eyes, a bright blue shirt and waiter's apron, grinned at this.

'It's OK. Dad isn't in this afternoon and anyway, haven't I always told you that his bark is worse than his bite? If he saw the three of you, sitting there looking all sweet and proper, good little Saint Jude's girls that you are, he'd be totally delighted that you're his customers.'

This made Amy laugh, along with Niffy and Min, her best friends and dorm-mates. The trio had been sharing a dorm at St Jude's ever since they'd arrived.

Gina, who'd only started last year, was the newest member of the dorm, the latest best friend and she was supposed to be here by now.

Dermot served them in order. First came sophisticated Amy, the one with the pretty face, groomed blonde hair and carefully chosen clothes. She got a skinny latte and a low-fat, wholemeal, pineapple and carrot muffin.

'Thank you,' she said, picking up her fork and considering which corner of the muffin she was going to dig into first.

'Min,' Dermot continued, looking at the Asian girl with the long dark ponytail and studious-looking brown eyes, 'you're a soya hot chocolate, because you don't get on with milk . . . and a blueberry muffin.'

'Thanks.' Min smiled. She had a big soft spot for Dermot. Until she'd met him and he'd been so friendly and chatty to her, she'd been terrified of boys. In fact, if it weren't for Dermot, she'd probably never, ever have even dreamed of going out with her lovely Greg.

'And this has got to be for you,' Dermot said to Niffy, as he put one huge, foamy cappuccino and a chocolate cupcake smothered in chocolate icing down in front of the tall and lanky, short-haired and scruffily dressed girl sitting between the other two.

Min looked a little longingly at the cupcake.

'It's not too late to change your mind,' Dermot told her. 'I'm willing and able. I can take the blueberry back to the counter and bring you a chocolate cupcake too.'

'No. No, it's OK,' Min decided. 'Niffy can eat all the chocolate cakes that she wants to because she played hockey all morning.'

'Too right,' Niffy declared, picking up her fork and diving in.

Dermot looked at his watch. 'Four o'clock already. Gina's late. Where is she, by the way? Did she not leave the boarding house with you today, then?'

'No . . . she had something to do in town. Maybe it was ordering up a new bit of games kit or something . . . I can't exactly remember.' Amy added carefully, 'You'll have to ask her when you see her.'

'She will be here, then?'

'Of course she'll be here,' Niffy added, voice thick with chocolate icing. 'Unless she gets run over by a bus, she'll be here.'

When Min saw the worried look on Dermot's face, she added soothingly, 'Gina has not been run over by a bus. She's just a bit late. She'll be here soon. Why don't you text her, see if she's on her way?'

8

'Maybe . . . right . . . I need to see to table seven. Catch you later.'

As soon as Dermot was out of earshot, all three girls looked at each other anxiously.

'I don't like covering up for her,' Niffy said.

'I hate it,' Min agreed.

'We told her today was the last day we'd do it. She's got to decide who she's going to go out with *today*,' Amy added. 'Lucky old Gina: struggling to decide between two guys, when I can't even find one.'

Both Niffy and Min looked at her sympathetically.

'It's OK for you two,' Amy continued.

'True for Min . . . but more complicated in my case,' Niffy said, then took a large slurp of cappuccino.

'Really . . . how are things?' Amy prompted, hoping to hear just a little bit more about Niffy and her occasional boyfriend Angus.

'Well . . . there's nothing wrong. But you know, when I see him it's great. When we're away at school, it's different. I don't want to do all that phoning and emailing and lovey-dovey stuff. I really can't be bothered. I think I liked it more when he was in France and hardly ever got in touch. I mean, I'm busy!'

Amy couldn't help laughing at this.

'What does Angus think?' Min asked.

'I dunno . . .' Niffy put the remains of the cupcake in her mouth. 'He probably feels the same.'

'So you're perfectly suited,' Amy said. 'Maybe you should just leave it like that. When you can see each other, have a great time. When you're apart, just . . . let it be. If it suits you both: fine. In fact, you and Angus are scarily suited. You'll probably end up getting married.'

'Amy!' Niffy protested. But she grinned anyway. It was quite nice to be told that she and Angus were perfectly suited.

'And here she is.' Amy was the first to spot Gina hurrying into the café with an expression of barely suppressed guilt across her face.

Gina rushed straight up to her friends first, without even looking around for Dermot. 'Where did you say I was?' she hissed at them.

'We told Dermot you were snogging the face off his best friend at the cinema,' Niffy teased.

Gina squeaked with horror at this.

'Adjust lipstick,' Amy advised, pointing to Gina's face where Mac's Lickable had been smudged all over the outline of Gina's shapely lips.

Gina gave another little scream and fled in the direction of the bathroom.

'There's a rash all over her chin,' Min added.

'Stubble burn,' was Niffy's verdict.

'How's she going to explain that away?' Amy wondered.

'We'll have to wait and see,' Niffy added, scraping a few remaining crumbs from her plate.

'Was that her?' asked Dermot, appearing at their table again. 'Where's she gone now?'

'Just making a trip to the little girls' room. Don't panic,' Amy told him.

'Well . . . not yet,' Niffy added in a low voice, but Dermot still caught it.

'What do you mean?'

'Hi, Dermot!' Gina hurried towards the table in a cloud of citrusy scent to cut off this line of talk.

She walked towards the four of them with a big smile across her face. Whatever she'd done in the bathroom in thirty seconds flat, it had worked: her smile was pink and perky once again, her red chin disguised with concealer. Any hint of another guy had been completely obliterated with a hefty dose of Gucci perfume.

The two-date outfit she'd so carefully considered this morning was still looking good: short orange miniskirt over black leggings and black ankle boots, with a shiny patent leather jacket on top.

Just like Amy's, Gina's hair was a bright, highlighted blonde, but whereas Amy usually wore her locks in a ponytail, Gina liked her hair to fall straight and loose down past her shoulders. Both girls had a strong sense of how pretty they were and they knew best how to work their looks.

'Dermot! I'm sorry I'm late, but it's OK, isn't it?'

Then, despite the crowded café tables, Gina and Dermot were kissing on the lips, maybe even with tongues – it was tricky to see from Niffy's angle, but she still couldn't help rolling her eyes at Amy.

Gina pulled back from Dermot to take a look at him. She'd been his girlfriend since last summer and now it was March. Nine whole months. Their eyes held each other's.

Gina really did like so many things about Dermot. He was funny. He was kind. He worked hard. He studied hard. He was super cute-looking too.

There was something between them. She felt the little buzz and tingle of attraction. There was definitely something there. But she knew now for sure that it was nothing compared to the electrifying jolt of being with Callum.

But Dermot was so nice. She hated that she had to let go of him.

'Hi,' he said, with his arm still on her shoulder. 'I was supposed to be free by four, but the girl doing the evening shift still hasn't made it here.'

'Oh no!'

Dermot reached over and kissed her on the lips again. 'I've phoned her and she'll be here soon. So, where are we going to go?'

'I was going to ask you the same thing.'

'Cinema?'

'No. I'm good,' Gina replied, just a little too quickly. 'I mean . . . I don't think there's much on that I want to go see right now.'

'Ermm . . . it's a bit early for something to eat . . . and I've had enough of cafés for one day . . . and it's too late to go to an exhibition or anything like that . . . ermm . . . do you want to come back to my house?'

Gina kept on looking at Dermot. Really, she knew she should tell him just as soon as she could that they were through. She was seeing someone else and not just any old someone else, but someone Dermot knew.

Callum and Dermot weren't best friends like Niffy had said. Whatever kind of friendship they'd once had had been destroyed when Gina had gone on a secret date with Callum the first time, and Callum just hadn't been able to stop himself from mentioning it to Dermot.

Gina had promised, sworn, absolutely insisted to Dermot that it was a complete mistake and it was all over. But that was no longer true.

With flirty emails and sweet-talking on the phone, Callum had won Gina over . . . because he was daring, he was fun, he was slightly outrageous and exciting to be with. Now, after her secret cinema date with Callum, Gina knew she had to finish with Dermot, no matter how awkward and upsetting it was going to be.

'I don't know . . .' she began. 'Hey, can we step outside for a couple of minutes?'

'Of course,' Dermot answered, and she saw the flicker of worry cross his face.

The café was up on the first floor above an art gallery, so once Gina and Dermot had gone out of the front door they were standing in a bright, white landing with stairs leading both up to the higher floors and down.

As Dermot pulled her close to him for another kiss, Gina said, 'I'm sorry, I can't . . . I'm really sorry, Dermot, but . . .'

She wanted to just say it straight off. Break up with him. Tell him it was over. Well . . . she thought she did. But when she looked into his face, then it was different.

14

Then she couldn't tell him, because she just wasn't sure anymore.

'I don't think I can come over to your house tonight,' she said instead.

'Why not?'

'Well . . . I'm supposed to be back at the boarding house by six-thirty. I don't have a late pass tonight and I have an English essay that's due in on Monday morning, so I'm going to be busy with that tonight and tomorrow . . .'

This was to put him off asking her out again on Sunday.

'Oh no . . .' Dermot repeated. 'We're not exactly having much fun, are we? I mean, when did we last go on a date?' Then, as they remembered the row about Callum, he added quickly, 'One which didn't go horribly wrong, Gina?'

She looked into his face and felt a fresh clench of anxiety in her stomach . . . Surely he didn't know about Callum? He hadn't found anything out?

Somehow the thought of Dermot knowing about her and Callum was even worse than the thought of breaking up with him.

'You do still want to go out with me, don't you?' He looked at her with a very serious face.

15

'Yes! Yes, of course,' Gina heard herself telling him, because she just couldn't bear to let him down. 'How can you say that after everything we've been through?'

'Phew! That's the best thing I've heard all day. All week, even.'

Chapter Three

Supper in the St Jude's boarding house on Saturdays and Sundays was never as good as any other night of the week, because it was made by the housemistresses, Mrs Knebworth and Miss McKinnon, instead of the boarding-house cook.

On Friday afternoons the boarding-house cook spent several frantic hours making Friday's supper as well as Sunday lunch, which she stored in the freezer before taking the weekend off.

So, after picking at some baked tuna-fish pie kind of thing, then eating a yoghurt, Rosie from Lower Fifth had gone up to her dorm to lie on her bed, read a book and eat her way slowly and carefully through a packet of Maltesers.

She was startled when Niffy, from the year above, knocked on the door, hurried into the room and went straight over to the window, turning the light out on the way.

'Hi,' Rosie said into the darkness. 'Is this about Mrs Knebworth, by any chance?'

'Yup,' Niffy answered, and she crouched down beside the window so she could look at the boarding-house driveway without being spotted.

Mrs Knebworth, the formidable boss of the boarding house, was a scary lady of about fifty-something who had been in charge for as long as anyone at St Jude's could remember.

She was the kind of short but completely solid Edinburgh woman who could stop a teenage girl in her tracks with a simple, but devastating, straight-lipped stare. With just a well-timed upwards flick of her eyebrow, Mrs Knebworth could extract confessions to crimes she hadn't even guessed at.

There were only a handful of girls in the boarding house who weren't secretly terrified of Mrs Knebworth, and Niffy was one of them. This was because Niffy had been in trouble with Mrs Knebworth so often and suffered so many of her worst punishments that the fear had gradually worn off.

The acutely interesting thing about Mrs Knebworth right now was that she actually seemed to have a *love interest*. On Saturday evenings nowadays, Mrs Knebworth no longer sat on the sofa in the sitting room, watching old films and making sure that girls got back exactly on time.

No, nowadays, more often than not, she left that job to Miss McKinnon. Mrs Knebworth, meanwhile, spent early Saturday evening getting ready to go out: a process involving brightly coloured frocks and blouses, vibrant pink lipstick, half a can of hairspray and a perfume so chokingly strong that girls who came within a few metres of her couldn't help coughing.

Then she was picked up in a blue Jaguar by a middle-aged man, always smartly dressed in a suit, who was related to her long-dead husband. Then, she was ferried off into the Edinburgh night.

She'd been spotted in restaurants – and even once at the opera. There were rumours that she was going to get engaged and be spirited away from the boarding house for ever.

'Don't you think it would be a good thing if Mrs Knebworth got married to Jaguar man and left?' Rosie asked, scrunching up the now-empty Maltesers packet.

'I don't know,' Niffy replied. 'She's the only house-mistress we've known. We could get someone much, much worse.'

'I think maybe you secretly quite like her,' Rosie dared.

For a moment or two Niffy didn't answer; she just carried on looking out of the window. But then, to Rosie's surprise, she replied, 'Maybe you're right. Maybe it's like when hostages fall in love with their captors. What's it called again?'

'No idea.'

'Stockholm Syndrome,' Niffy remembered with a satisfied smile. 'Yup, I've got Stockholm Syndrome. Mildly, obviously. I'm not in love with the Neb, or anything. Here he is, bang on seven-thirty, the Jaguar man.'

Rosie couldn't resist it; she had to sneak over to the darkened window too and take a peek.

The housemistress, wearing shiny pumps and a trench coat buttoned up against the chilly March evening, came out to the driveway, waved, then got into the door opened by the man in the suit.

'I think he's called George Arbuckle,' Niffy whispered, 'and I just can't shake the feeling that I've seen him somewhere else. In some sort of . . . I don't know how to put this . . . but a bad situation.'

'What do you mean?' Rosie asked.

'I recognize him from somewhere. And it's not a good place. It's a bad-vibes thing.'

'I think you're just imagining it. Look at them having

a little laugh together. He seems perfectly nice.' But when the middle-aged couple kissed quickly on the lips in the front seat, Rosie couldn't help making a squeak of disapproval. 'Do you think they'll get married?' she asked Niffy.

'Who knows? He must be covered in pink lipstick now.'

'Nah, Mrs Knebworth's a blotter. Her lipstick lasts for weeks.'

'Huh?'

'Never mind. What about Gina?' was Rosie's next question.

'I don't think *she's* about to get married.'

'No. That's not what I meant. Has she chucked Dermot yet?'

'No. She was supposed to do it today. But apparently she lost her nerve. Or her horoscope said she couldn't . . . or whatever excuse it was this time. I can't even remember.'

'Who do you think she'll choose? Callum or Dermot?'

'Who knows?' Niffy repeated. 'She's in our dorm right now discussing it to death with whoever can bear to keep listening.'

* * *

21

When Rosie tapped on the door of Iris dorm, the room shared by Gina, Niffy, Amy and Min, two voices told her to come in.

Opening the door, she saw that both Gina and Min were there. Gina was cross-legged on her bed, brushing her blonde hair. Min was folding her way through a pile of laundry on her bed.

'Rosie, hi! How is my favourite little Lower Fifth?' Gina gushed and stretched out her arms to give Rosie a hug, then a little air kiss on the cheek.

'Hello,' Min offered; she was friendly, but not as lovey-dovey as Gina.

'I'm just talking it over with Min,' Gina said, expecting Rosie to understand what she meant straight away. 'I *still* don't know what to do.'

'Poor you,' Rosie said, perching herself beside Gina on the edge of her bed.

'Dermot is a really, really nice guy, Gina,' Min said, shaking out a pair of pyjama bottoms, all crinkly and crunchy because they'd been hanging in the drying room for too long. 'You really like him, he really likes you. I'm sorry, but it's a no-brainer. You two should stay together. You should just put Callum right out of your mind and be glad that Dermot has too.'

Gina sighed and carried on brushing.

'Min's probably right,' Rosie offered.

'Probably...' Gina said, but she sounded very uncertain.

'What's so great about Callum anyway? And wasn't he going out with someone in the Sixth Form?' Min asked.

'Milly – that is definitely finished. He told me himself, plus I heard some of her friends talking about it. What you need to understand is that Callum,' Gina went on, 'is just much, much more exciting than Dermot.'

There was another tap on the door and Mel, from the year above, came into the room.

'Gina?'

'Hi.' As Mel stepped into the room, Gina had to add: 'You look amazing.'

Mel flashed a quick smile at the compliment. She was all set to go out, her skinny legs outlined in spray-on shiny black leggings, a black lacy minidress on top and the highest-heeled dark green mary janes on her feet.

'How are you going to get out wearing that?' Min wondered.

'The Neb has left the building,' Mel said, applying lip gloss with her fingertip, then smacking her lips down on top of it. 'Gina, I was just wondering if ...'

'You could borrow my eyeliner again?' Gina guessed.

'Yes, please,' Mel said. 'I spent ages looking for one just like it today, but nothing comes close.'

'Must be a special US edition.' Gina rummaged in her top drawer and brought out the dark, shimmery inky-blue eye pencil which Mel couldn't party without.

'Where are you going, Mel?' Rosie asked.

'Clubbing,' Mel replied, 'but it's down on the permission sheet as birthday party and overnight stay with best day-girl friend, Isla. You have to make some really good day-girl friends,' Mel advised, 'otherwise you will never, ever have a good night out in this town. So, have you got rid of your loser waiter yet?' She stopped applying liner for a moment and glanced over at Gina.

'That's not very nice,' Min protested.

Gina shook her head.

'Why not?' Mel wanted to know. 'The entire boarding house is talking about it. Probably the rest of the school is too. I'm amazed *he* hasn't heard about it yet. You'd better hurry up or he'll know more about it than you do. Loads of Saint J's girls go to that café and someone is bound to talk.'

'I really like him ... and I really like Callum too. I can't decide.'

'Oh, just move on! Honestly, you're fifteen. There are so many great guys out there,' Mel promised, bending forward to study her eye-lining handiwork in Gina's mirror. 'It's Saturday night and you're sitting in your dorm in your trackie bottoms. Are you staying in to do homework with Min?'

Gina nodded.

'See, this is why you need to ditch Dermot and move on. You should be out tonight doing something else that is a lot more fun.'

Chapter Four

On Sunday night, Amy emptied her purse and counted out her money to see how much damage she'd managed to inflict on her funds over the weekend.

OK, she'd been working at her part-time job as a shop assistant for most of the day on Saturday, so she'd made £45, which would come to her in a few weeks, but then she'd had coffee and cake, bought a new lipstick, paid for a taxi back to the boarding house . . . *eek!* She'd spent £24.40 and now there was only a fiver and some coins left.

'Oh no,' she said out loud, but it was still to herself, as no one else was in the dorm right now. She looked across the top of her chest of drawers. Where once there had been expensive fancy-label creams and make-up, there were now products from Superdrug, The Body Shop and Boots. Plus, Amy's jewellery box was emptier than it had once been.

Her once very wealthy dad was going through a lot of business problems and Amy had promised to pitch in and help him out just as much as she possibly could. If he had to scrape together money to pay her boarding-school fees, then she'd told him she could earn her own pocket money and get by without any of the luxuries she'd been so fond of in the past.

She'd given some of her best jewellery back to him to sell. She'd even put many of her loveliest clothes on eBay and she'd had to somehow cope when her dad had packed up their lovely flat in Glasgow and put it up for rent.

The situation was still not good, but her dad kept promising her that in just a few months' time it would all start to look better once again. In the meantime, Amy was just about managing on her no-luxury diet. She still had a very posh bottle of perfume left, half full, and whenever she felt too down in the dumps about being much, much poorer than in the past, she squirted a little blast onto her wrist where she could sniff at it for the rest of the day and remind herself that the good times were certain to come back again.

The door opened and Gina walked into the room. When she saw Amy's money carefully laid out on the bed, looking as if it had been recently counted, she immediately offered: 'If you need a loan for something, you just have to ask.'

Amy smiled and shook her head. 'No debts. But it's nice of you to offer, anyway.'

'How's it all going ... financially?' Gina asked the question carefully. Amy hadn't spoken about her dad's business for a while and Gina hoped this wasn't because things were bad.

'My dad keeps saying lots of reassuring things,' Amy began, 'but I can't help worrying. I mean ... he's working really hard, building his business up again. But if things go wrong, I know I'll have to leave the school ... and that would be really hard.'

'Try not to worry,' Gina said sympathetically. 'It might all work out just fine and you'll have wasted lots of time stressing.'

Amy pushed a smile onto her face. 'You're right. You're totally right. How's the essay coming on?' she asked, wanting to change the subject.

'Finished.' Gina managed a smile. 'But I still haven't made the Big Decision.'

'The Boyfriend Choice? Oh for goodness' sake! You're going to have to stop or you're going to drive us all *bananas*. Look, shall I just take Dermot off your hands?' Amy joked. 'That will solve everyone's problems because then I'll have a boyfriend, Dermot won't be sad and lonely and you'll be free to snog Callum until your chin is raw.'

'Very funny. But would *you* go out with Dermot . . . if I wasn't going out with him?'

'No. Not my type. I like them tall, dark, very handsome and completely uninterested in me. That is my type. Jason, you'll remember . . .'

'How could we forget?' Gina said with a roll of her eyes. 'Jason, who turned out to be dating some model-a-like at the same time as you.'

'Yeah . . . the boy with the gazelle on the side. Then there was Finn . . .' Amy trailed off.

'What did happen with Finn?'

Finn was Niffy's big brother, and for a few weeks Finn and Amy had looked like one very hot item, despite Niffy's complete disapproval.

'I dunno, really. It just seemed to fizzle out.' In dramatic voiceover mode, she added: '*They laughed, they kissed, they promised to keep in touch . . . And she never heard from him again.*'

'Amy?' Gina gave her friend a very serious look. 'Honestly, right down in your heart of hearts, what do you think I should do?'

'Ha! You're asking *me*? When I'm just desperate to be

with whoever will have *me*!'

'Don't say that. You are very special. Only someone very special will do for you.'

'Sometimes you are just too Californian to be true, Miss Very Special.' Amy smiled, sat down on the edge of her bed and gave Gina and her problem full attention. She spoke seriously now. 'You like Dermot, but you don't like him enough to stop liking Callum a lot. Right?'

'Ermm . . . I think so.'

'So, I think, to be fair to Dermot, you have to let him go. You don't want to stop seeing Callum, do you?'

Gina shook her head.

'And Dermot is far too nice to cheat on, agreed?'

Gina nodded.

'So there you are. You have to let Dermot go. Even if it's really painful.'

Chapter Five

'Good morning, girls.'

The headmistress of St Jude's, known to just about everyone in the school as Banshee Bannerman, looked down from the stage at her 430 day girls and boarders with her usual bright, brisk enthusiasm.

'At the start of the summer term, we're going to hold a charity fundraising month here at Saint Jude's. We all need to think of those who are not as fortunate as we are. This year, I have decided to delegate. I want *you* to come up with wonderful ideas for raising money and even more wonderful ideas for where to donate it.

'We'll do this as a competition. The best fundraising idea earns an extra hundred pounds for the charity of their choice.'

Niffy glanced sideways at her friends. 'For the Banshee that is generous and almost quite nice,' she whispered under her breath. 'What's come over her?'

'What's her idea of a good cause, though?' Amy countered. 'Latin teachers in distress?'

This made both Gina and Niffy, who were on either side of her, start to giggle.

Min, who liked to keep to all the school rules, even the one about silence in assembly, nudged Niffy in the ribs.

The Banshee held forth about public duty, civic responsibility, good citizens with charitable intentions and then it was time for the morning's prayer followed by the morning's hymn. Finally a chorus of scraping chairs and footsteps meant it was time to head for lessons.

Someone was loudly telling their friends: 'We are so going to win this competition with my genius idea. We are so definitely going to win! Oh, look, it's Amy McCorquodale . . . are you going to set yourself up as a charity? Then maybe your friends could try and raise some funds for you?'

Amy didn't have to turn round to see who had made this casually cruel remark. She recognized the sneering voice straight away.

Penny Boswell-Hackett was a day girl in Amy's form; she was in Amy's English class, in Amy's French, history and maths classes too. Unfortunately, Penny also played hockey in the A group, along with Amy, Niffy and Min.

For reasons established way back when Amy was brand-new to St Jude's, Penny saw herself as Amy's enemy and took every opportunity that she could to tease Amy, make fun of her and generally put her down.

But Amy always stood up for herself. She knew that Penny was just a mean snob who shouldn't be allowed to get away with any of the things she said.

Now Amy stopped walking and turned on her heel, even though this meant holding up the whole line of Upper Fifths trying to exit the assembly hall.

'Did you just call me a charity case? Someone who needs my friends to raise funds for me? Did I just hear you properly?' she snarled.

'You don't need to look so surprised,' Penny snapped back. 'Everyone knows your dad's gone bust and you'll only be here till the last of the money runs out.'

For a moment, Amy just gasped. This was so mean and nasty, it was like a bucket of icy water landing on her head. 'How dare you, Penny Boswell-Hackett?' she hissed. 'How dare you? You are the biggest cow I have ever, ever had the misfortune to meet, and as for calling me a charity case!! You know what? I am going to come up with the biggest, best fundraising idea you've ever heard of and it will wipe the floor with yours.'

Amy turned and hurried away, before Penny could take the astonished look from her face and think of something even more horrible to say back.

As Niffy settled down at her desk beside Amy for the start of their first class, she couldn't help telling her friend: 'OK, so that's just great . . . you've thrown down the challenge and all we have to do now is think of the biggest and best fundraising idea anyone's ever heard of. Don't suppose you've got any suggestions?'

'No, not really,' Amy admitted.

Chapter Six

Min filed into the biology lab with a bundle of books and papers under her arm and a heavy school bag over her shoulder. In the summer, she'd sit exams in nine subjects.

She and a handful of other very clever Upper Fifths were the most overworked pupils in the entire year. But Min liked it that way. She loved to learn and she had big, big ambitions.

Her parents were both doctors in her home country of South Africa and they were sending Min to the best school they could afford in the hope that she would get into medical school and follow in their footsteps.

Min loved the idea of helping people and she was really good at science, but unfortunately she just didn't think medicine was going to be her thing, because whenever she saw blood she fainted.

But this didn't make her feel any less ambitious. She dreamed of going to one of the best universities and becoming a world-famous researcher.

'Are you giving your talk today?' her friend Zarah asked as soon as she walked into the room.

'No!' Min looked at her in surprise. 'No, I'm Wednesday. I'm sure I am. I mean, I've written my talk but I'm not ready to give it yet.'

'OK, no worries. I was just asking if it was your turn.'

'Is it yours?'

'Yeah . . . I'm a bit nervous, though.'

'Don't be silly, you'll be fine. This is Mr Harrington's accelerated learning group. All his students get As.'

'Do they?'

'Apparently so. Apparently he just doesn't accept anything less than your best work. Plus he's such a good teacher, everyone does really well.'

'Wow.'

Mr Harrington came out of the lab's supply room and walked down to the front of the class. 'Hello, Upper Five.'

He was a small man with a ginger beard and heavy glasses. His woolly tie and jumbo cords looked a bit shaggy and beardy as well. His white lab coat was a little too big for him and he kept having to push up the sleeves.

'So, I have three names on my list of girls who are going to give talks today . . . Yes, Asimina?'

Min put her hand down and asked Mr Harrington the question she'd been longing to ask ever since she'd read his degree qualifications. 'Mr Harrington, is it true that you went to Cambridge University, sir?'

'Yes, Asimina. A long, long time ago now. Probably before you were even born,' he joked, causing a light ripple of giggles, because despite the shaggy clothes and the beard, he was still youngish, maybe around the thirty mark.

'So you must be really clever, because it's very hard to get into Cambridge, isn't it?' Min went on.

'Well . . . I suppose, yes, it's quite hard. It depends what subject you do, though. I mean, if you wanted to study Ancient Greek, you'd probably find it's not too difficult to get into Cambridge. But maths, for instance, that's hard. For a start, you're competing against all the brilliant Taiwanese students.'

Another light giggle rippled through the room.

'Did you do biology?' Min asked.

'Natural Sciences, yes.'

'So, how did you get in?'

'Well . . .' Mr Harrington paused for a moment and scratched his head. 'I studied hard, I got good grades, but I think it was because I had a real passion for the subject. A university like Cambridge has so many great students to choose from that they pick the people who really eat, sleep and breathe the subject they want to study. They choose the students who spend their spare time reading more and more, working on extra projects and discovering just as much as they can about it.'

This was provoking groans from some parts of the classroom. But for Min it was very interesting information. She wanted to go to one of the famous universities. She wanted to be able to look at her parents – who'd spent so much money on her education – one day and be able to tell them: 'Mum, Dad . . . I got into Cambridge.'

It would be the ultimate.

'Do you think anyone you're teaching at the moment is good enough to get into Cambridge?' Min asked, her voice faltering a little. It was so weird to hear herself say out loud, for the very first time, the thing she wanted most in the world.

'Well, Asimina . . .' Mr Harrington paused. He gave her a long look.

Min felt her heart speed up a little. Was he about to

name her? Was he going to tell her that already he thought she might be good enough to go?

'There are a lot of very clever, very hard-working girls right here in this class and you're one of them. You should all set your sights high and aim to do really well. But I think it's a little too early to tell where you'll be going to university. Asimina,' he reminded her, 'you've not even taken your Standard Grades yet.'

Chapter Seven

It was noisy and cosy in the boarding-house dining room that evening. Despite the heavy rain lashing the big windows, the lights were lit and the warmth of a room filled with eighty chatting, gossiping, bickering voices kept the bad weather at bay.

'What are you doing at Easter?' Gina was asking Niffy.

'Staying at home, riding Ginger, studying for my exams. Same old boring stuff as just about everyone else, I think,' Niffy told her. 'Oh, happy days, it's steak pie,' she added, as the oven dishes with the main courses were brought down to the long tables.

'What about you, Amy?' Gina wondered.

'I'll be in Glasgow: studying in the rain and hopefully working at one of the River Island shops there, part-time. I'm going to get my Edinburgh boss to put in a good word for me. But totally jealous of you and Min going home to the lovely warm spring sun of California and . . . ?'

'Durban,' Min reminded her. 'It'll be autumn there. But still warm.'

'What is Durban like? I can't really get a picture of it in my mind.'

'It's a big, busy city with a beach. I'll show you photos upstairs after supper if you like . . . but really, you should come and visit.'

This made Amy smile. 'Thank you! I can't tell you how nice that would be. But the current state of finances . . . '

'I know,' Min said gently, not wanting Amy to have to spell it out.

'What's the gossip?' Rosie leaned over from her seat several places down to ask.

'Just discussing Easter holidays,' Amy answered.

'I think you mean Easter study leave,' Min corrected her.

There was the sound of a glass being *ting-ting*ed with a spoon and Mrs Knebworth stood up at her head table in the large bay window at the end of the room.

'This is it,' Niffy hissed. 'She's about to announce her engagement.' Many heads snapped in Niffy's direction, followed by whispered comments:

'No!'

'You're joking!'

'No way.'

'Have you heard?'

'It must be love. She even looks younger.'

'You're a nutter!'

'Good evening, girls, I hope you're enjoying your delicious supper,' Mrs Knebworth began. 'I know that Mrs Bannerman told you all about the fund-raising month at assembly this morning. Wonderful news. I want everyone to have a think about how the boarding house can work as a team to raise money for a good cause. I'm going to put a suggestions box out in the hall and everyone with a good idea can drop it in: either with your name on the suggestion, or if you're modest, without. Thank you.'

'Phew!' Niffy said, once Mrs Knebworth was back in her seat. 'I heard that Jaguar man has popped the question and Mrs K is currently considering. Look how cheerful she is . . . she's smiling, not scowling, and so far this term she hasn't told me off for anything. A record.'

'Who told you about her engagement?' Amy asked, eyes now widening with interest.

'Well . . . not exactly a reliable source,' Niffy had to admit.

'Who? Oh, not Mel?'

Niffy nodded.

'You can't believe anything from Mel.'

'But it's obvious the Neb is enjoying herself, and she does look younger. She's even bought herself those trendy glasses.'

'Yes, I know, but it's only been a few months. *The Neb* is hardly going to rush into getting married, is she?'

'But Mel said—'

'Never mind what Mel said. By the way, have you heard what happened to her?' Amy gave a tiny point in Mel's direction.

Niffy, Gina, Min, Rosie and everyone else within earshot looked over. They could see Mel from behind. She seemed to be sitting very stiffly upright; she also looked much wider than usual.

'Back brace,' Amy said, spooning a small mound of mashed potato onto her plate, as she enjoyed being the centre of everyone's rapt attention. 'When she was out clubbing on Saturday in those really, really high boots she was wearing . . . well, spiky heel met damp Edinburgh moss. She skidded up into the air and fell right down six very large, very cold stone steps. Landed on her bum.'

'Ouch,' Min sympathized.

'You are a good person,' Amy told her. 'Apparently Mel has cracked her coccyx, slipped some sort of disc and will have to wear the brace for three weeks.'

'Yikes, that puts an end to her Saturday-night street-dancing,' Niffy added.

In a tiny whisper, Amy also had to say, 'Not to mention her s.e.x. life.'

'Where else are we going to go for our information?' Niffy wondered.

'*Cosmopolitan*?' Gina suggested.

'Maybe you could write to the problem page and ask them if you should dump Dermot?' Niffy chipped in.

Gina shot Niffy a glare. 'Very funny. It's OK. I've decided what I'm going to do.'

Chapter Eight

The following Sunday, Gina dressed up carefully and thoughtfully. She pulled on her nicest jeans and a bright, silky top. Then came boots, a fitted jacket and a woolly snood to keep the weather at bay.

She applied berry-coloured lipstick and a little flick of waterproof mascara, then put in her favourite earrings shaped like silver leaves.

Finally there was a little squirt of perfume.

She wanted to look nice, but she didn't want to look too adorable. Just normal nice would be fine. She braided her hair into a loose plait, then looked at her watch and realized it was time to go.

She was supposed to meet Dermot at the Modern Art Gallery at 3 p.m. It was already 2.40, and if she didn't leave now she would have to run most of the way to be on time.

But before she left, she had to find Amy and just go

through it with her once again, so she hurried out of the dorm and down the many flights of stairs to the Upper Fifth common room where she hoped to find her.

As she opened the common-room door, several heads turned in Gina's direction.

'Hi,' she said, spotting Amy, 'can I talk to you for a minute?'

'Sure,' Amy said, patting the arm of the sofa she was sitting on.

'No. In the corridor. It's private.'

'About you going off to ditch Dermot?' one of the other boarders asked. All the other girls in the room laughed. 'It's about as private as the size of Mrs Knebworth's nose,' the girl added. 'Don't be surprised if there are spectators at the art gallery café.'

'Amy!' Gina exclaimed. 'How *could* you tell everyone like this?'

'I didn't tell everyone. Everyone knows! You must have told some people, and you know what this place is like – it's spread like wildfire.'

Gina was so annoyed at this she slammed the common-room door shut and stomped down the corridor to the housemistress's sitting room. Anyone going out of the boarding house had to get

Mrs Knebworth's permission in advance, then sign out and back in again under her or Miss McKinnon's watchful eye. There were many things which sometimes made the boarding house feel like prison. This was definitely one of them.

'Ah, Gina,' Mrs Knebworth said, lowering her newspaper as Gina came into the room.

'I'm just heading out to the Modern Art Gallery to meet Dermot for an hour or so, remember? You said that would be OK.'

'Oh dear, Gina . . .' Mrs Knebworth shook her head.

'What?'

'Dating is delightful, but breaking up is never easy. Good luck.'

Gina's mouth fell open with surprise. Everybody knew. Every single person knew. This was a nightmare. What if she got to the gallery and suddenly felt just as crazy about Dermot as she had when they'd first started going out? Then everyone would keep asking why she hadn't dumped him. And what if he got to hear about her plan?

What if he already knew?

This was horrible.

She scribbled her name onto the sheet, then left the room without another word.

'I'll expect you back by six at the latest, and there's no need to be huffy!'

Mrs Knebworth's words rang in Gina's ears as she opened the big wood and glass door, closed it behind her and ran away from the boarding house as quickly as she could.

The further she got from the boarding house, the closer she got to the art gallery. Now this began to feel much more real and much more nerve-racking.

She was going to break up with Dermot. For real.

There had been a break-up a few weeks ago, but it had only lasted for a few hours before they'd got back together again. But this was really going to be goodbye.

She couldn't help thinking of all the good times they'd had together. Now that she was going to finish things, her brain was reminding her of:

Dermot joking with her mom, even though all his jokes fell flat.

Dermot kissing her for ages and ages when she was supposed to be helping him with his history revision.

Dermot's mum, Dermot's house, Dermot's ever-ready smile, Dermot's way of making almost everything seem funny.

Dermot turning up at the Halloween party dressed as Shrek! How could she forget about that? How could she dump Shrek?!

She knew she'd love to keep Dermot as a friend. But that was going to be impossible. Especially if she dated Callum.

Dermot and Callum were at school together and Dermot would know all about Callum's new girlfriend. So Gina and Dermot couldn't be friends. This was definitely going to be goodbye.

She began to walk up the long driveway to the art gallery, wondering if she would get there before him. Just the thought of what she was going to have to say to him was making her heart skip about in her chest.

Walking into the café, Gina realized it was busy. For a moment, she scanned the packed tables and didn't think that Dermot was there. But then a wave caught her attention.

There he was!

She couldn't help herself from smiling and there was a burst of feeling pleased until she remembered just what she was here to do.

As she passed through the tables towards him, Gina was not exactly over the moon to see Rosie and two of her friends drinking tea and sharing a piece of chocolate cake at a table just two down from Dermot's.

'Hi,' she said, almost under her breath, when Rosie looked up and saw her.

'Oh . . . hi . . .' Rosie said and began to blush.

She knew! She knew why Gina was here. No doubt about it.

Gina looked away from Rosie and focused on Dermot, who was walking over to her.

'Hello, gorgeous, how are you doing?' he greeted her. His smile was totally friendly, totally welcoming. He held out his arms and Gina leaned down into them, accepting the hug and the kiss on the lips. 'Tea? Coffee? Hot chocolate? Or something wild and wacky, like maybe chai?' Dermot asked.

'Chai would be good . . . but can we get it to go? It's so hot and busy in here . . . maybe we could walk round the sculpture gardens outside.'

'Scene of our first kiss. Can I just remind you of that?'

'No! Our first kiss was in my car on the way to the airport.'

'Oh, you're right. How could I forget? But the sculpture gardens was the scene of our first official date kiss.'

'No it wasn't! I think that was at your house . . . never mind . . .' Gina felt flustered. 'OK. We've kissed in the sculpture gardens before. Does it matter?'

'Of course it matters. It all matters. The little things matter. Let me get your tea.'

'No, it's OK, I'll get it.' Gina was desperate for Dermot not to pay. She couldn't make him buy her an expensive cup of tea and then dump him once she'd drunk it. 'I'll get the tea,' she insisted. 'Would you like something?'

'Well . . . maybe a paper cup so I can take my coffee outside with me.' He pointed at the elaborately creamed and sprinkled drink in front of him.

'Sorry, do you mind?' she asked.

'Not really.'

Once she was in the cool, fresh air of the gardens, away from the stares of the Lower Fives, Gina began to calm down. She had her tea in one hand and Dermot's fingers in her other.

As they walked along, he chatted about the café and how his exam revision was going. He was hoping to do well enough in his summer exams to get into Edinburgh University.

Exams . . . and working in the café. That was all Dermot had time for right now. She was amazed he'd even managed to get away to meet her here. That was a big part of the problem.

He was lovely, but compared to Callum . . . he was a little bit boring.

'So . . . how are you?' He turned, smiled and fixed his blue eyes on hers. As soon as that happened, Gina felt herself wavering.

'Well . . . well . . . the thing is . . .' She wished she'd done this by phone. Or email . . . or even sent him a text.

But nine months! They'd been dating for nine months. She couldn't just end that with a text.

'The thing is . . .'

They had stopped walking now and were standing, facing each other. Dermot was still smiling, with obviously no idea what was coming next. A pained expression was beginning to take shape on Gina's face.

She had watched the break-up scene on so many films and TV shows, but she'd never actually done this. Well, OK, they had sort of broken up before, but they got together again immediately afterwards.

This was the real thing.

She was about to really, really hurt and reject him. It felt very hard, especially when he was looking at her with his lovely smile, expecting her to tell him something much more ordinary.

'The thing is . . . the thing is . . .' she stumbled, 'we're going to have to break up. This is the thing . . .' Her voice sounded all choked and anxious. 'We're going to have to break up because . . .' She looked down at the grass and the pointy toes of her boots. 'Because I really like you, Dermot' – she clung onto his hands tightly – 'but I don't want to go out with you any more.'

There. She'd said it and she knew he'd heard it because there was a stunned silence hanging between them. She dared to look up into his face and felt an immediate pang at the hurt she'd caused.

It took him several moments to find his voice.

'Well . . . I'm . . . I'm a bit surprised,' he spluttered. 'I mean, we've been through this. We did break up and you convinced me you'd made a terrible mistake. You convinced me, and now you're doing it all over again.' His voice seemed to range from choked to hurt, to angry and back again. As if he couldn't decide how he was supposed to feel.

'I'm sorry. I really like you, Dermot. I really do.' Gina searched his face. This was true. This really was true; she could feel an ache building up in the back of her throat. 'But . . . I don't want to be your girlfriend any more. I want to . . . move on.'

Ouch. That seemed to land like a slap on his face. He winced.

'Dermot, you're a great guy. Really, really great . . .'

'But not great enough for you?' He made a bitter little half-smile, which disappeared as quickly as it had come. 'Please tell me you're not going out with Callum? Please tell me I'm not being dumped for *him*?'

Gina bit her lip. She didn't dare to lie to him because she knew he would find out.

'Oh, great! That is just great. Just what exactly is so . . . so . . . fascinating about Callum? He's an idiot, you know. A total idiot.'

She carried on biting her lip. Nothing she could say would be good enough.

'Well . . . you just go off . . . with Callum then. I hope you have . . . have a . . . a . . . lovely time.' Dermot sounded an almost perfect mixture of angry and upset. His words were stuttering out awkwardly.

'Dermot, please . . .' Gina said, feeling tearful and confused. 'I don't want to hurt your feelings.'

'Well then, stop dumping me every five minutes.'

'But I don't want to do this any more, even though I really like you.'

'Are you sure?' He stepped close to her, took hold of her upper arms and searched her face.

Looking into his face made her feel overwhelmingly sad, overwhelmingly sorry for him, but Gina still nodded.

Yes. She had really, really liked him. But it was time to move on. Otherwise what? There was no one who didn't go through break-ups. Otherwise, everyone would be happy ever after with their first-ever boyfriend.

'I really liked you,' she said. 'You made me very happy. You were part of the reason I came back to Edinburgh. But now, we're back to friends. I hope . . . I really hope we can be OK with that. I couldn't bear to lose you as a friend too.'

'When you break up with Callum,' Dermot said darkly, 'you can come and see me in the café any time.'

She leaned over, wanting to kiss him once more, aiming for his lips. But he turned his head and the kiss landed awkwardly on his cheek.

He began to turn away. He was going. This really was the last of Gina-and-Dermot. She felt a horrible stab of sadness.

'Take care,' she said in a little whispery voice.

Dermot's phone began to bleep. He pulled it out of

his pocket. 'That'll be my new girlfriend,' he tried to joke, but his voice sounded gruff and not at all funny. He called up the message, then just stared at it with a surprised look on his face.

'Is everything OK?' Gina asked.

'Nice of you to have told everyone you were going to dump me,' Dermot said bitterly.

'What do you mean?'

Dermot held up the phone so she could read the message: POOR YOU. I THINK YOU'RE LOVELY XX

'I didn't tell—' Gina began, but stopped right there, because she had. 'Who sent that?'

'Caller withheld,' Dermot told her.

Chapter Nine

'Aim! There you are!'

Niffy rushed into the St Jude's boarding-house laundry room, brandishing a letter in her hand. Amy was sitting on top of a table eating a Pot Noodle while Min tried to put up the rickety boarding-house ironing board.

'Is that a Pot Noodle?' Niffy asked, stopping in her tracks. 'Can I have some? In fact, have you got a spare one? I am *starving*. We had double games and the new woman, Miss Jonker, made us run around the pitches six times to warm up.'

'No, I haven't got any more and no, you can't have some of mine,' Amy said, pulling the pot towards her protectively.

'What is so great about those things, anyway?' Min asked. 'They taste horrible.'

'Give me that,' Niffy told Min. 'The great science and

maths brain of the twenty-first century unfortunately can't make any sense of an ironing board.' As she went over to help Min, she put down the letter she'd been carrying on the table beside Amy.

'So what is this? Is this what's got you all excited?'

'Yeah,' Niffy said, putting the ironing board up in a moment, then coming back to study the contents of her letter with Amy.

Amy picked up a newspaper cutting and glanced it over. There was a picture of a horse receiving a third-place rosette. 'Is that Ginger? The horsey love of your life?' she teased.

'Yes. He's being ridden by this friend of mine during term time, she took him to a show and they did really well. And that's why Mum sent me the cutting from the local paper. But that's not why I've been running all over the place trying to find you . . . Look on the back.'

Amy turned over and saw the headline: THIRD COURT APPEARANCE FOR MAN ACCUSED OF OAP FRAUD. Beside the story there was a black-and-white photo of a man in a suit hurrying down the court steps.

'So?' was Amy's reaction. 'I don't get it. Do you know an OAP he's defrauded?'

'No! But I know *him*! We *all* know him.'

Amy looked at the photo much more carefully now, and Min even left her ironing to come over and take a squint.

'That is Mrs Knebworth's boyfriend!' Min was the first to gasp.

'You are joking!' Amy exclaimed, pulling the paper closer.

'Not this time,' Niffy said. 'Of course it is; it's Jaguar man. Are you going blind, Amy? I knew I'd seen him somewhere before and it says in this story the paper covered his last two court appearances.'

'What's he supposed to have done?' Min asked.

'Cheated five OAPs out of their life-savings with some dodgy financial scheme. Basically, Mrs K is dating the Bernie Madoff of Cumbria.'

'You have got to be joking,' Amy repeated, but seeing the picture and skim-reading parts of the story, she knew that it was true.

'Mr Edward George Arbuckle; that's his name, isn't it?' Min asked. 'I've definitely heard Mrs Knebworth talk about "Georgie" and Miss McKinnon referred to him as Mr Arbuckle.'

'Do you think Mrs K knows about this?' Amy asked. 'I mean, he's supposed to be her late husband's cousin ... or do you think he lied about that too?'

Niffy looked at Amy, then Min in turn. 'If you think the Neb, the pinnacle of respectable Edinburgh society, knows that she is dating someone who makes court appearances charged with OAP fraud, then you can't know her as well as I do,' she replied.

Min and Amy exchanged a glance. This was totally true. There was no way the Neb knew.

'Oh no! With her lipstick and her floral numbers and her Saturday nights at the opera, she's having so much fun,' Min began. 'Niffy, you just can't want to be the one to tell her!'

Chapter Ten

Something had also arrived for Min in the post that day, but as she didn't think her dorm friends would be interested, she kept it to herself.

She came back up to the dorm after she'd finished her ironing and the angst-ridden discussion with Niffy and Amy, in which they'd decided Niffy probably should tell the Neb about Jaguar man, but maybe not yet.

Sitting on the chest of drawers beside Min's bed was the cardboard box filled with bubble wrap which contained the brand-new laboratory standard microscope which her dad had sent her. Her parents seemed to be gradually resigning themselves to the fact that if she went into medicine, she'd probably go into medical research rather than patient care, so maybe that's why her dad had sent the microscope.

Min carefully lifted the bubble-wrapped weight

out. She'd already inspected it, but now she was actually going to prepare a slide and look down the lens at it.

She looked around the dorm, wondering what she could use. The Iris dorm (all the boarding-house dorms were named after flowers) was a cosy attic room filled to bursting with four beds, four chests of drawers, a small wardrobe and all the many, many belongings of four girls.

Family photos and posters hung on the walls. The dressing tables were cluttered with hair products, face creams, make-up brushes and jewellery stands, and the chairs at the end of every bed were draped with clothes. Under every bed there was an untidy jumble of sports kit and shoes: multicoloured pumps, heels, patent leathers and tennis rackets under Gina and Amy's beds; muddy boots, schools shoes, trainers and hockey sticks under Niffy's.

When Min's eye fell on Niffy's trainers, she remembered with a jolt that summer term and athletics were coming, and she'd hardly done any training at all the whole winter. She considered scraping some mud from Niffy's boot for the slide, but she didn't think that would be interesting enough.

Min went over to the little attic window and there

she found exactly what she was looking for: a small, dead hoverfly trapped in the little bit of spider web in the very corner of the window. She borrowed tweezers and a pair of nail scissors from Amy's chest of drawers, plucked the fly from the web and began to snip it into tiny pieces over her slide. Then she added a drop of saline solution and pushed the other slide on top, making a glass hoverfly sandwich.

As soon as she'd switched on the microscope and focused in on the slide, she couldn't help giving a 'Wow!' out loud because she felt so excited by what she could see.

'I love bugs,' she whispered to herself. 'I absolutely love bugs.'

There was a knock on the door.

'Come in,' Min answered.

A girl from two years below, one of the more shy new girls, was standing there looking totally out of breath.

'Are you Asimina?' she asked.

'Yes. Hi.'

'There's a phone call for you.'

'Thanks, that's so nice of you to come all the way up here and get me.' Min remembered just how annoying it was to be a junior in the boarding house and have to run about answering phones, finding people and taking messages. 'Do you know who it is?' she asked, hurrying to the door.

'A guy . . . I think he said his name was Greg.'

'Greg!' This spurred Min into excited action. 'Thanks!' she called again as she raced across the landing, out of the fire door and began to take the steps two at a time.

Greg had been Min's *boyfriend* – she still felt a tingly thrill at the word – since Christmas. Her very own, very first boyfriend. Greg was completely and totally cute, and just to prove how much they had in common, they'd met through an online physics homework club.

Min raced down the many flights of stairs, then dashed along the corridor, worried that he might have given up waiting for her on the other end of the line.

'Hello?'

'Min – is that you?'

'Hi! How are you?' Min settled herself on the little stool in the cupboard with the phone, and she and Greg chatted about school, about homework and most importantly, about films they might like to see at the cinema next weekend.

'Hey, I got a microscope!' Min told him. 'A real one, electric, lab standard with slides and a light and everything.'

'A microscope?' Greg sounded surprised. 'What are you going to look at with a microscope?'

'Everything. Anything and everything. I'm going to look at whatever I can jam in between two glass slides.'

'What are you looking for, Min?'

'I don't know ... exactly. But that's what good scientists do, don't they? They just keep looking and looking at things until they discover something.'

'Sounds a tiny bit madly obsessive to me,' Greg teased. 'Is this to do with your long-term goal of getting into Cambridge?'

'It was a present,' Min reminded him.

'OK. But I think we'd better go and see something really dumb at the weekend.'

'Greg, do you think I'm smart enough to get into Cambridge?'

'It's going to be really, really hard for you to get into Cambridge, Min.'

'Why?!'

'Because you'll have to compete against some really, really smart people ... like me!'

Chapter Eleven

'Have you read this book?' Amy asked Gina, pointing at the copy of *To Kill a Mockingbird* on her desk.

'Yeah, it's great. The whole Southern accent thing is fun too. You should definitely go for that.'

They were in Mrs Parker's English class where they were supposed to be choosing books for their personal study essays. 'Quiet discussion' was allowed.

'Girls,' Mrs Parker said as a light warning when Penny B-H burst into another fit of giggly laughter at something her friend Louisa had said.

Louisa and another girl, nicknamed Tiggy, had been Penny's best friends for as long as Amy could remember. Amy had always called Tiggy and Louisa 'Piggy' and 'Weasel' behind their backs.

'What do you think they're so excited about? The copy of *Oliver Twist* in Penny's hands? I don't think so.'

'Maybe they've thought of some fundraising ideas,'
Gina suggested.

'Bet they're better than any we can come up with,'
Amy said glumly.

'Have you even tried to think of any?'

'Well . . . not exactly. Sponsored run?' she suggested.

Gina wrinkled up her face. 'I dunno. It's not the most
original and it doesn't exactly sound like fun. I mean,
a run? Plus you'd have to run really far to impress
anyone, now that practically everyone's mom is running
a marathon. You'd have to run three marathons in a day
or something.'

Amy gave a sort of disgruntled 'hummmpff' at this.
'Well, what about you? What have you come up with
then?'

'I don't know yet,' Gina answered, 'but I'm thinking
about it . . .'

'I'm amazed you've got time to think about anything,
what with your two boyfriends.'

It was Gina's turn to scowl. 'That's not true,' she
snapped. 'I finished with Dermot on Sunday, you know
that.'

'But I also know he's left two messages on your phone
since then.'

'I've ignored them,' Gina told her, but coloured up.

'How do you know? Someone texted him to commiserate about two minutes after I gave him the news. Was that you, by the way?'

'No, of course not,' Amy said, looking surprised. 'I just heard about his messages from Niffy, because you told her.'

'Oh, yes,' Gina remembered.

'Someone texted him just after you dumped him?'

'Girls . . . are we staying on the subject of good books?' Mrs Parker fired the question in their direction.

Gina nodded in reply.

'No idea who it was?'

'He showed me the text; no name, and number withheld. But whoever sent it knew that I was there to finish with him.'

'Well . . . to be fair, quite a lot of people knew about that,' Amy pointed out.

'Even Mrs K!'

Amy pressed her lips together to stop herself from laughing out loud.

'She wished me luck and said breaking up was hard to do!'

'Oh, that's bad,' Amy sympathized.

They felt Mrs Parker's eye upon them once again and

turned to the little pile of books on their desk.

'*The Curious Incident of the Dog in the Night-time?*' Gina picked the book up. 'Cool cover,' she said.

'Cool book,' was Amy's verdict. 'Try it.'

As soon as Mrs Parker had moved on to another part of the classroom, Amy had another not-exactly-book-related question for Gina.

'If we were going to do a fundraising thing, which charity would you want to raise funds for?'

Gina thought for a long moment. She tapped her pink pencil against her lips, then decided: 'Orphans. I'd want to give the money to orphans. I hate it when they do news reports from foreign orphanages and you see all those kids looking totally lost . . .'

'Yes. Even worse, when there's a disaster,' Amy whispered, 'and they show the kids who've just been orphaned. That is horrible.' She squeezed her eyes shut against the thought.

'So orphans it is, then,' Gina said.

'Yes. Do you think we feel so sorry for orphans because of our parents?'

For a moment Gina didn't say anything. She knew, of course, that Amy was talking about the parents missing from both of their lives.

Gina had her mom and her stepdad, Mick, but she

hadn't seen her real dad since she was seven years old. When she was little, she'd asked her mom about him a lot. But it had been a long time now since she'd raised any questions.

Amy's situation was more extreme. She had a young dad she was very close to and a gran. But her real mum hadn't been around since she was a baby. Amy's mum had been just seventeen years old when Amy was born, and she'd apparently not been interested in her baby for long.

'Maybe . . .' Gina said thoughtfully. 'But it's not like I miss my dad. I'm just kinda curious . . .'

'Don't you miss him at all? You must remember stuff about him.'

'I guess . . . well, maybe I just haven't thought about him in a while. Maybe I should think about him . . . I don't really know,' she sighed.

'I think it must be lovely to have a mum,' Amy said, 'but a nice mum, who cares about you . . . not the kind of mum who'd give you up as a baby and never get in touch with you again. I mean, what kind of mum is that?'

'Do you think you'll ever get to know her?'

'Girls!' Mrs Parker's voice was raised now, she

was looking directly at Amy and Gina. 'Unless you'd both like to write me a very long essay on Dostoyevsky's *Crime and Punishment*, you need to concentrate on what we are supposed to be doing. Right now!'

Chapter Twelve

CALLING GINA CALLING GINA. THIS SHD PROB BE MY LAST
AND FINAL TXT. U R SURE. YES? IF SO I NEED 2 MV ON.
DERMOT X

Gina stared at the words on her phone screen for a
long, long time. They made her want to cry. But she
was sure. She was definitely sure. Dermot was a lovely
guy and she had been totally crazy about him for a
while. But it was over. No matter how many cute texts
he sent.

The feeling of needing to cry was building up in her
chest. Gina looked around the dorm where Min was
totally engrossed in her microscope and Niffy was
sitting on her bed reading a riding magazine. There
wasn't exactly much privacy in here.

She got up and headed towards the bathroom. But
there the four cubicles with gaps under the doors just
weren't private enough to cry in either.

Gina tried the handle on the small room with the bath, but an irritated voice called out: 'Engaged! Like it says on the door!'

Now she really wanted to cry. Now she could feel tears welling up behind her eyes, making them hot and stingy. She wished and wished that she was at home. There she had a bedroom all to herself and a huge bathroom with a walk-in shower. If she was at home, she'd be able to cry and cry herself to pieces on her lovely big bed, then she could step into the shower and wash it all away.

Gina began to walk down the stairs, thinking vaguely that she would head in the direction of the Upper Fifth common room. Maybe it would be quiet in there and she could have a little sob.

The weather seemed to know just how she felt. Passing a window on the stairway, she saw rain splashing against the glass and now she had another reason to feel sad. In California, it would be spring, with warm heat from the sun, people wearing white jeans, thinking about sandals, putting on wetsuits to swim in the sea.

Standing just outside the Upper Fifth sitting room, Gina could hear laughter coming from inside. Girls were in there chatting, drinking cups of tea and exchanging the latest news. Gina heard the very infectious giggle of Serena and it made her feel better.

She turned up the corners of her mouth and was just about to push open the door and join them when the mobile in her hand burst into life. The ringtone let her know that home was calling.

'Hi, Gina.'

'Mom!'

'I know I should not be making transatlantic calls on the cell phone, but I had to tell you . . .'

With the phone pressed to her ear, Gina hurried along the corridor, looking for a quiet corner to enjoy this conversation. There, the window was set back from the corridor in a slight recess; no one was hanging about there right now, so she took up the space.

'Mick and I have landed an amazing new deal. A really very amazing deal,' Gina's mom, Lorelei, told her in the sophisticated English-meets-California accent she'd developed over the years. 'It's even better than we'd hoped for and, baby, it's all signed up and definitely going to happen.'

Gina could hear how excited her mom was. Mick and her mom ran their own software company and to Gina it felt like they'd been doing great for years now, but she could still remember way back when she was small how business had been more of a struggle for her parents then.

'Wow, that's fantastic, Mom. I thought the last deal you did was going to set you guys up for years to come and now there's another one?'

'We've made it, baby,' her mom said in a voice that was hushed and a little breathless with excitement. 'This time we've really made it.'

'Have you made enough money to last, like . . . for ever?' Gina was whispering too, because she didn't want anyone passing through the corridor to hear.

'We will personally make about fifteen million dollars with this new deal. So yes, it could kinda be enough to last for ever, provided we don't start buying helicopters or desert islands or that kind of thing.'

'That is amazing . . .' Gina had to pause to let this really sink in, but it just didn't, not really. 'Will you retire?' she asked her mom, smiling slightly because she'd already guessed at the answer.

'I don't think so!' Her mom laughed. 'I'd be too bored. But I do want to treat you and Menzie to something wonderful, because I know it's been hard for you when Mick and I have been working like crazy.'

'Like a holiday?' Gina wondered.

'I don't know yet. Menzie says he wants us all to go to

Alaska. He wants to visit some place where bears roam the high street!'

'Cool!' Gina had to admit her little brother could really come up with the wacky ideas.

'So maybe we'll have to go visit Alaska some time . . . but what about you, Gina, what's your idea of a dream holiday?'

Gina thought.

She looked out of the window. It was a grey-skied day and rain was still smacking angrily against the glass. Her idea of a perfect holiday was to go home: to be with her family in the sunshine, in all the comfort and familiarity of home . . . to see her old friends again.

There couldn't be any way to make a holiday more perfect – could there?

'Mom?' Gina asked, suddenly struck with inspiration. 'Could I invite Amy, Niffy and Min to come home with me?!'

Chapter Thirteen

'What did they say?' Gina asked as soon as Min walked into the dorm, but she could already tell by the smile on Min's face that the news was good.

'They said yes!' Min exclaimed. 'I still can't believe it!' Min had just finished the phone call with her mother and rushed straight up to the dorm to tell the others.

Amy and Niffy had both been able to get hold of their parents yesterday, when Gina had shared her mom's amazing news and invited them all on an all-expenses-paid visit to California. But Min's parents had been out, so she'd only been able to contact them this evening.

'So we're all going?!' Amy said, just to be sure.

'Looks like it,' Min replied.

'We are all going to be boarding a jumbo jet and flying off to the sunshine just as soon as this term finally ends? Unbelievable!' Amy added.

'Hug!' Gina instructed Min, who looked so astonished and excited she was in danger of bursting into tears.

'I was just so sure they would say no,' Min said. 'They only get to see me in the holidays, so I didn't think they'd let me go and stay with you for a week. It's so exciting!' she exclaimed, accepting Gina's offer of a hug.

'Group hug!' Gina instructed, so now Amy, then Niffy joined in, just briefly, until Niffy announced: 'C'mon. This is totally soppy. We may be going to California, but that doesn't mean we have to turn into tree-hugging hippie types.'

'You're really going to come with us?' Amy directed the question at Niffy.

Niffy raised her eyebrows. 'I know. Shocking. I've never been on a plane journey that took longer than two hours.'

'Long-haul,' Min corrected her. 'You've never flown long-haul.'

'Whatever.' Niffy shrugged. 'But once I'd made it clear, for the fourth time, that the shaky Nairn-Bassett finances were not going to be stretched, thanks to Gina's incredibly generous offer, then yes, they were happy to let me come along.'

'It's not my offer, it's my mom's,' Gina reminded them.

'Yeah, but you could have chosen anything you wanted and you wanted us to come to California with you!' Amy reminded her. 'That's just incredibly generous. I don't know if I'd have done the same for you!' she added cheekily.

'What would *you* have asked for?' Gina directed the question at Amy.

But both Min and Niffy chorused together with her: 'Jewellery!'

'Am I that predictable?' Amy wondered.

'Yes!' Niffy and Min said together.

'I might have chosen some amazing clothes.'

'And jewellery,' Niffy said.

'Anyway . . . it's going to be warm and sunny over there – hard to believe,' Amy said, pointing at the window where another dark and damp evening was beginning to settle in. 'Have you thought about what to pack?' With this, she opened the drawer that was closest to her and had a rummage around inside. 'Not too bad,' she declared. 'When I was in Dubai with Dad last year, I got lots of lovely summer things.'

Niffy groaned and threw herself down on her bed. 'Oh, great . . . I usually spend all summer in my jodhpurs and school hockey tops. I have about zero summer clothes and a budget of zero.'

'Your *school* hockey tops?' Amy repeated in disbelief.

'Don't worry,' Gina hurried to reassure her, 'it's not going to be really hot. Just a nice warm, spring kind of weather. You can wear jeans. I've got a whole wardrobe at home you can borrow from. Really, it's not a big deal.'

There was a brisk knock, then one of the girls from the year above stuck her head round the door.

'Gina Peterson?' she asked.

'Yeah. Hi.'

'I'm really sorry, but this is for you. I misread the name and only realized when I'd opened it up.' Gail Petherton handed a small padded envelope over to Gina. 'Really sorry.'

'No worries,' Gina told her.

'I haven't taken any, I promise,' Gail added, 'but I am jealous!' She closed the door, leaving the four girls to wonder what was inside the envelope.

Gina put her hand in and drew out a folded sheet of paper, then she reached back inside and found a handful of sweets. 'Ooooh!' She went to her bed and tipped the envelope out. A tumble of US candy fell onto her duvet cover.

'Nice. From home?' Niffy wondered.

Gina looked at the sheet of paper. 'This is just one of those print-out invoices. I can't see a name . . .' She scanned the sheet once again. 'No . . . maybe Mom or Mick sent them and just forgot to put their name in. Have some . . . just make sure there's some Reese's Pieces left for me, you know how much I love them.'

The other girls didn't need to be asked again to make a selection.

Niffy was holding up a mini chocolate bar and asking, 'Tootsie Roll? Will I like this? What does it taste like?'

'You'll love it,' Gina told her.

Min picked out something for herself and wondered, 'Do you think this could be from Dermot?'

'Why wouldn't he sign his name, though?' Amy asked.

'No . . .' Gina said thoughtfully. 'I'm kind of sure it's not Dermot. I think he knows we are really through.'

'Shame . . .' Niffy said. 'I really like Dermot. But not as in . . . you know.'

Gina didn't reply. She turned to her bed and looked at the candy that was left. Her hand went immediately to the orange and brown Reese's Pieces wrapper. She was going to eat one of these first.

She'd never told anyone part of the reason why she liked these chocolate and peanut butter treats so much: it was because of her real dad.

Although she'd not seen him since she was seven, Gina still had a few vague memories. One of those memories was sitting beside him, on Halloween, after they'd toured round the neighbourhood houses. Together, they'd looked through her candy bag and he'd picked out one of these and shared it with her.

When she got back to California, Gina was going to ask her mom if there was any way of getting back in touch with her dad.

Chapter Fourteen

'Girls!! You made it! How fantastic to see you!'

Gina was doing a double take. Her *mom* was here at the airport to pick them up? This was unbelievable. How had her mom managed to find a break in the hectic Lorelei Winkelmann schedule to drive over to the airport and meet Gina, Niffy, Min and Amy off their flight?

'She's so gorgeous,' Amy whispered to Gina. 'How can you stand it?'

'I know,' Gina sighed.

Lorelei was a too-glamorous mom. She had a toned, worked-out figure, she wore beautiful clothes, her hair was pulled into one of those perfect up-dos, even her shoes were just the exact kind of not-too-high but totally elegant action-girl heel which everyone wanted just as soon as they saw them.

'Wonderful to see you!' Lorelei exclaimed, scooping

each and every one of them in turn into her arms for a hug and a kiss. 'You must be exhausted.'

Now this was true. The flight from London had taken thirteen hours, and they'd travelled down from Edinburgh four hours before that. But Gina had found travelling in a group much more fun than travelling alone.

Each member of the foursome had approached the journey in their own unique way.

Min, a practised long-haul flier, had drunk bottled water and nibbled apples and nuts in-flight. She'd come with her own eye mask and blanket, and managed to sleep for most of the journey.

Niffy, who'd only been on four plane rides in her entire life, had found everything the most exciting thing ever and had just about driven them insane:

'Look at this TV!'

'Look at the choice of films!'

'Look at this tiny bag of nuts!'

'We can drink as much coffee as we want!'

Causing her friends to finally beg the air hostess, 'Please don't give her any more!'

Amy, also a seasoned flier, had approached the long hours in the departure lounge in exactly the same way as Gina: a chance to catch up on the latest make-up, perfume and beauty news. By the time Amy and Gina had made it onto the plane, they'd been trailing clouds of perfume and had the weird smudgy look of customers who've been treated to one too many makeovers.

'We are tired,' Gina told her mom.

'No we're not!' insisted Niffy, who had definitely overdosed on the airline coffee. 'This is so exciting! I don't want to sleep. I don't want to miss one minute of it.'

'Are you driving us?' Min asked, looking quite calm and refreshed after her long nap.

'Yeah. Grab your bags and we'll load up the car. The traffic's terrible in the city, but once we get onto the coast road you're gonna love the view.'

Gina sat in the front passenger's seat of the sleek silver convertible, beside her mom so they could catch up with news. But she kept getting distracted with the excited chatter coming from her friends in the back of the car.

'Palm trees!!' (Niffy)

'Look! A pink limousine! Do you think that was someone famous?' (Min)

'Did you see that woman walking into that shop? She had six little dogs.' (Niffy)

'Look at these shops! They are amazing. Did you see all the bling in that window?' (Amy)

'We just drove past Tofu Hut? Please promise me we're never going there!' (Niffy)

'Gina! Are you listening to us or are you texting Callum?' Amy asked.

'Both,' Gina replied, her phone in her hands.

'Callum?' Gina's mom asked. 'Do I know about Callum?'

'Just ask us,' Niffy piped up, 'and we'll tell you everything you need to know.'

Finally they were out of the snarl of early afternoon traffic and onto the highway which took them north of Los Angeles and towards the beautiful seafront town of Malibu, where Gina and her family were lucky enough to live.

As the wind whipped at their cheeks and hair in the roofless car, Amy and Min gazed at the endless blue sky and ocean through sunglasses. Niffy just clamped her hand above her eyes and squinted out at the sparkling view ahead of them.

It was a long drive from the airport to Malibu, but as the views just seemed to get better and better, everyone relaxed and enjoyed the ride.

'There are forests!' Min exclaimed from the back seat. 'I wasn't expecting forests.'

'Yeah, not far north of where we are you can go hiking through the redwoods.'

'Redwoods!' Min and Niffy both repeated with excitement.

'What's a redwood?' Amy wanted to know.

'The biggest tree on the face of the earth. Like the dinosaur of the tree world,' Min explained.

'But not extinct, obviously,' Niffy added, 'so number one adventure activity: hiking through the redwoods.'

'Noooo!' Gina and Amy protested together.

'I bought six different swimsuits,' Amy protested, 'and nothing to hike in at all. I didn't know about hiking. I don't want to go hiking!'

'Number one adventure activity will be attending Paula's pool party and meeting her gorgeous new boyfriend and his many talented friends,' Gina turned from the front seat to tell them.

'Now that sounds more like it,' Amy agreed, 'but does Callum know?'

'Shut up about Callum!' Gina protested.

'*We'll* go hiking,' Niffy assured Min.

'Wow, look at the size of that place!' Amy pointed to

a white house rising like an elaborately iced wedding cake from succulent grounds where palm trees and cactus plants were fighting to escape.

'Welcome to Malibu!' Gina called to them from the front seat of the car. 'I think you're gonna love it.'

'We already do!' Amy shouted back, and as Gina's mom slowed the car down to a more sedate town-centre pace, Amy flung open her arms, hanging one out of the open car and repeated: 'We already do!'

It was the very beginning of April, but already there was a summery, seaside feel to the place. The special smell of sea air hung over the streets; people were casually dressed, almost always in jeans, trainers and sunglasses.

Lorelei turned the car left, then wound down several side streets, bringing them closer to the sea. She slowed up outside a pair of wrought-iron gates, then brought out something which looked like a tiny TV remote and clicked it. The gates bleeped and then began to slide slowly open.

'Awesome!' Niffy declared. 'Maybe we could persuade Mrs Knebworth to get some for the boarding house . . . to keep out all the "unsuitable young men".'

This made everyone laugh.

The car pulled in through the gateway and now

Gina's friends were straining to take in all the details of this amazing house all at once.

The garden was all smooth jewel-green lawns and manicured shrubbery. In fact, there was a gardener wearing a wide-brimmed sunhat clipping away at something right now. The driveway opened out to a sunny, paved courtyard with a fountain in front of the house – and then there was the house itself.

'Wow!' was Min's reaction, which pretty much summed up everyone else's feelings.

The house was a beautiful dazzling white and glass modern creation; it looked absolutely huge. The windows on the ground floor alone looked about five metres high.

'You didn't tell us you lived in a palace,' Niffy said to Gina.

'Hey, I've seen your house. It's not exactly small,' Gina reminded her friend.

'But my house is falling down,' Niffy said matter-of-factly. And this was sort of true of the crumbling, ancestral Blacklough Hall, which had been in the Nairn-Bassett family for generations.

'Shabby chic,' Gina said.

'But your house is totally shiny, new and beautiful,' Niffy told Gina and her mom generously.

'Thanks. C'mon, grab your bags, I can't wait to show you round.'

'And where is the swimming pool?' Min wondered.

'It's round the back. Much more private like that. You're going to love it!'

Lorelei popped open the trunk of the car and everyone scrambled for their bags, shaking off any sense of tiredness because this was so exciting.

Gina led them into the white perfection of the entrance hall where their feet tappity-tapped against snowy marble tiles. Before they could say anything about how impressed they were, there was a sort of half-shriek, half-whistling sound, and a boy with overgrown curly dark hair whizzed at high velocity down the marble staircase and landed in a heap at their feet.

'Jeeeeeeeez, Menzie, please stop skateboarding down the stairs,' Lorelei complained. She'd entered the hall just in time to see this minor disaster.

Menzie picked himself up. He looked cheerful and slightly embarrassed. 'Nope ... nothing broken,' he assured his mom. 'Gina, hi. Gina's friends, hi.' He gave a little wave and looked up at them through his thick fringe.

'Hug,' Gina instructed.

Menzie gave a little shrug of his striped T-shirt, which looked about four sizes too big for him, and obliged. 'Hi,' he repeated, and shook everyone else's hand in turn till he came to his mom.

'Pick up your skateboard and tidy away, then you can join us out on the terrace for some tea and cake,' Lorelei said with a smile.

'Cake!' Both Menzie and Niffy said this word at the same time with an equal amount of enthusiasm.

'But you have to see your rooms first,' Gina insisted.

'Yes, sure, go upstairs, freshen up and I'll see you out there in twenty,' Lorelei told them.

The bedrooms were just as amazing as they might have expected from what they'd seen of the house so far. Amy was going to share with Gina, sleeping on the huge spare bed which pulled out from under her pink and white princess creation. Min and Niffy were sharing the room next door, where a vast king-sized bed had been made up for two, complete with separate duvets.

'The view is amazing,' Niffy enthused, marching straight over to the window and pulling it wide open so she could drink in the blue of sea and sky.

'You have to come and see Gina's private bathroom,'

Amy said, bursting into their room. 'I think we can safely say we'll be teasing her about this for ever!'

Now everyone had to hurry into Gina's room to inspect the bathroom.

'It's not that bad!' Gina said defensively.

Min and Niffy's reaction was yet another gasped: 'Wow!'

It was so big. It was so fancy. It was so *pink*!

'Gold taps,' Amy pointed out gleefully.

'It's a fantastic shower,' Gina said, a little huffy. 'When you stand under that, you'll wish you had one just like it at home.'

'Oh God, yet another thing for me to feel jealous about,' Niffy groaned. 'I already want to swap homes, families and, in fact, just about my whole life with you!' This made everyone giggle.

'Go change out of your sweaty stuff, then we'll go down and have tea, then a swim,' Gina told them.

Gina, her mom, her brother, Amy and Min were all sitting around the pretty white table beside the swimming pool when Niffy made her entrance.

'Oh!' Gina couldn't help exclaiming at the sight of her. 'Whoa! What a . . . a . . .'

'Good idea,' Min finished the sentence tactfully.

Niffy was standing in the doorway in a tiny swimsuit. It wasn't just tiny – about three sizes too small – it was also oddly grey-looking. It had clearly once been striped white and pale blue but it had obviously been in the wash so many times that it had become blue and dingy grey. Niffy had a bony body and a flat chest, but the swimsuit looked stretched to its limit across her frame. If she'd had big boobs, they would hardly have been covered.

She looked surprised to find no one else in a swimsuit, but just whipped the towel from her shoulder and wound it around her waist to cover her up while they had tea.

'Have a seat,' Lorelei said, offering Niffy the chair next to hers.

'Thanks. Are we actually having tea? Not coffee?'

'Proper British tea, yes. I know I sound almost completely Californian now, but I'm still half Scottish and I went to Saint Jude's, so I do know how to make tea.' She picked up the large white teapot and began to pour out Min's cupful.

'The cake looks sensational,' Niffy approved.

In the centre of the table was an elaborate tart decorated with all kinds of different fruit, which were laid out in beautiful circles and covered with a sparkling glaze. Lorelei cut out generous slices for the four girls and Menzie, but only took a small sliver for herself.

'Is there cream?' Menzie wanted to know.

'Do you have to?' Lorelei asked.

'I guess . . .' Menzie replied.

'OK, go get it from the refrigerator.'

Menzie shot off from the table and was back moments later with a great big aerosol can full of cream, which he was shaking heartily. He set it down on the table in front of him and got back into his chair.

'Would anyone else like some whipped cream? It is really, totally yummy. Excellent with this cake.' He looked at Amy, who was sitting opposite him and held out the can. 'Just try a little. It's delicious.'

Amy smiled at him. 'Thanks,' she said. 'OK, I'll take a little squirt; it's been ages since I used one of these.' She took the lid off the cream can, put her finger on the nozzle and turned the can upside down.

'Hold it right down on the cake,' Menzie instructed.

Amy pushed and with a loud *whoosh*, a huge jet of cream blasted out of the can, bounced off the cake and squirted straight onto her new silk top.

Amy shrieked.

Min gasped.

Gina and Lorelei both shouted: 'Menzie!!'

Menzie doubled up with laughter and Niffy reached over to examine the can. When she saw that it was still squirting, she realized that the nozzle had been tampered with.

She looked over at the creased-up Menzie and realized she had found a true partner in crime.

Chapter Fifteen

'There they are! Look over there!'

The excitement in Gina's voice was obvious. A big grin spread across her face.

Amy, Niffy and Min, sitting beside her in this very air-conditioned branch of Starbucks inside this completely air-conditioned mall, looked up and saw the three girls they recognized as Gina's Californian best friends walking towards them.

Paula, Ria and Maddison looked just as cool, pretty and sophisticated as you'd expect a trio of fifteen-year-olds from the West Coast to be.

Paula was black, although the word hardly did her silky, coffee-with-cream coloured skin justice. Her fine, crinkled hair radiated out from her delicate face like an afro halo. On either side of her were Maddison, a sun-kissed blonde, and darker-haired Ria. All three were dressed in a selection of denim jackets, skimpy scarves, multicoloured minis, leggings, sneakers, a jangle of bracelets, necklaces and neon nail varnish.

They swooped down on Gina and her St Jude's friends, who found themselves caught up in cherry lip-glossed hello kisses and a whole scented cloud of hair products and perfume.

'Hi, guys!' Paula said with a big smile. 'Great to see you all again.'

Last year, Paula and Maddison had travelled all the way to Scotland with Gina's mom. They'd met Gina's friends, toured around Edinburgh and even made a trip to a Scottish island.

'You're on *our* home ground this time,' Maddison added. 'This is Ria. You didn't get a chance to meet her. So here she is. Meet Niffy, Min and Amy.'

Ria found some more chairs, so all seven girls could crowd around the small table.

'How are you? How is everyone? Give me all the news,' Gina insisted.

'Paula will start by telling you all about her *New Boyfriend...*' Maddison began.

Cue much giggling and Paula rolling her eyes.

'Oooooh, and then Gina will tell you all about bye-bye, Dermot... hello, Callum,' Amy added.

'Oh no!' Paula exclaimed. 'I luuuuved Dermot.'

'I'll go get drinks . . . the usual, P and R?' Maddison asked. 'Anyone else want anything?'

'Tell . . . tell everything,' Gina said, fixing her eyes on Paula. 'You tell me everything about your new boyfriend, then I'll tell you everything about mine.'

Amy and Min looked interested too, but Niffy pushed her chair back from the table and said, 'I'm doing another bun run. Anyone want anything?'

'*Eeeek!* Are you joking?' Amy asked. 'Swimsuits, Niff, got to think of swimsuits.'

'Talking of swimsuits—' Gina began, but Niffy was already gone.

'The lure of the carrot cake is too strong,' Amy explained.

'Back to the boyfriend news, please,' Gina insisted.

'OK, you know him . . .' Paula began.

Gina gave a little shriek of anticipation.

'But don't judge me. Do not judge me. He's in the year below us . . .'

Gina shrieked again: 'Ohmigod! It's Larson, isn't it? Please tell me you are dating Larson.'

Paula nodded.

'Ohmigod! He's like the best-looking guy in the entire school. You two must look like a Benetton ad.

I mean, he is so blond and so . . . buff,' Gina added, very impressed.

'Uh-huh,' Paula agreed.

'Is he fourteen?' Min asked.

'No! Well, he's going to be fifteen tomorrow. That's why we're all going to his party.'

'Really! Larson is having a party and all the cute guys from his year will be there?' Gina said, looking significantly at Amy.

'Some people from our year too. He wanted to make sure we all felt at home.'

'Really?! Who's coming?' Gina asked, eyes wide with excitement.

As Paula went through the list of names with her, Min turned to Ria.

'Hi,' she said in her quiet, sweet way. 'How's your sister doing?'

The reason Ria hadn't been able to come to Scotland last winter was because her sister had been very ill, in hospital with an eating disorder.

'That's really nice of you to ask,' Ria replied. 'She's been home for four months straight now. No dramas, no hospitalizations. She's doing OK. You should see our kitchen, though, and our meals. We are talking uber, uber healthy.' She tucked a wisp of straight brown hair behind her ear. She was a slight girl with pale eyes and pale skin. Separated from the jangly glamour and good looks of her friends, she looked much more ordinary than them. 'My mom had this idea that if Megan wouldn't eat our kind of food ... and every single meal was a war zone, let me tell you,' she continued, 'then we should start eating her kind of meals. So we're practically vegan now, and I thought it was going to be the worst thing ever, but it's kind of OK. Megan was so amazed by us, so impressed that we loved her enough to do this ... I mean even my dad, who is like totally Mr Meat, is eating tofu and nut roasts – it's really helped her to get better.'

'That is so nice of you,' Min said.

'Well ... Dad and I do sneak out now and then for a burger, but I think that's OK. The main thing is, Megan is getting well and she's much happier. We had to get her well. It was terrible last year ... I thought she was going to die ...' Ria's eyes suddenly welled up. She brushed the first hint of tears away with the back of her hand and immediately apologized.

'It's OK. Really, it's fine,' Min said, and patted Ria soothingly on the arm.

'Hey, you,' Gina said, looking at Ria, 'are you OK?'

'Yes,' Ria said, putting a smile onto her face. 'Things are going much better.'

Maddison came back with three iced shakes which she put down on the table with the words, 'It's warm enough to stop drinking coffee, yay! I can't stand coffee, even with like five packets of NutraSweet.'

Niffy returned with a huge slice of carrot cake. 'Don't even think about asking me for a bite,' she said, especially to Amy, as she put her hand around her treat. 'If you want, you'll have to go get your own.'

'OK, so pool party at Larson's tomorrow, starting at five o'clock. You can all come, can't you?' Paula wanted to know.

'Yes!' just about everyone chorused back.

'Min?' Gina asked.

'Well, I suppose I'll give it a go. I like to swim,' she added.

'Please tell me that just as soon as we've finished our drinks we are going to do a little shopping,' Maddison said. 'I have a really cute dress I want to wear tomorrow, but I definitely, definitely need a new bikini.'

'Bikini? You're obviously feeling brave. I'll be the girl in the swimsuit and matching sarong,' Gina told them.

'Why?' Paula asked, eyes wide. 'You have a great body.

I have big buns, you have big boobs, Maddison has sticky legs – who cares? It's all about celebrating diversity, didn't you know?'

'My boobs aren't big!' Gina protested.

'My legs aren't sticky!' Maddison declared.

'Who cares?' Paula said again. 'If you don't love your own body, who else is gonna?'

'Yeah, we'll go shopping. We'll help you find the perfect bikini,' Gina told Maddison.

'Not me,' Niffy said through a full mouth. She began to shake her head.

'Why not?' Ria asked, although the St Jude's girls already knew the answer.

'Severely limited funds,' Niffy replied, and gave Ria a wink. 'Enough to buy the odd bun or two. But nothing that will stretch any further.'

'Niff . . . I don't know if your swimsuit will stretch any further,' Amy warned.

'Well . . . Niffy . . . I've got something I want to say to you about that . . .' Gina began. 'Look, I've got a whole drawer full of swimsuits and bikinis, really. I don't wear most of them, so if you'd like to borrow, that will be just fine. You're only a little taller than me, so I'm sure you'll find something.'

'That's very kind of you,' Niffy said. Accepting an

offer like this without any protest let everyone know that Niffy must understand how tiny and kind of shocking her own swimsuit looked.

'But . . .' Gina went on, and she looked up at Niffy with something of a mischievous smile, 'there's something you'll have to do first. I can't let you go to a pool party without this.'

'Huh?' was Niffy's response.

Gina looked at her watch. 'I've made you an appointment. In about fifteen minutes. I'll take you there; it's a really nice place. And cheap. There is absolutely no need to freak out.'

'Huh??!!' Niffy repeated. She was beginning to look worried.

'Niffy, I'm sorry, it's not just that your swimsuit is small. You also need to have a bikini wax.'

Niffy gasped and promptly began to choke on a crumb of muffin. She coughed, spluttered and Min finally had to pat her on the back. 'I'm fifteen!' Niffy declared. 'I'm too young!'

'You are nearly sixteen,' Gina said firmly, 'and you are way too hairy for the state of California.'

'Yeah,' Paula agreed, 'the swimsuit police might come and get you!'

Chapter Sixteen

'So you tie the string round the handle like this, then you loop it through here and you make sure your knots are really good and tight. They've got to be able to take the strain.'

Niffy was concentrating so hard on this job that she did not notice at all the look of pure admiration on Menzie's face.

She had already showed him how to leave jam-jar lids screwed on so lightly that when anyone picked up a jar by the lid, they were rewarded with an instant crash, bang and splatter of jam.

Now Niffy was instructing her adoring young pupil in the art of fixing a door. The one they'd chosen was Gina's bedroom door.

Revenge definitely had to be taken on Gina. Niffy had practically been frogmarched by Gina and her friends to the waxing parlour the day before.

Having boiling hot wax poured on the very top of your legs, at the side of your pants, then ripped off . . . was about as painful as Niffy had expected it to be. However much she might appreciate the smooth, still-pink and pimply skin when she'd tried on Gina's cherry-red swimsuit later, Niffy still didn't think it had been worth the pain.

'So, why have we tied up her door so that it only opens some of the way?' Menzie wanted to know.

'OK . . . this is the point where we close the door, hide in this doorway right here – with this door open just a peep – then call for Gina.'

'Really?'

'Yeah, give her a shout. Tell her you're looking for something in her room – that'll get her up here quick enough.'

Menzie went to the top of the staircase. 'Gina!' he yelled out.

No reply.

'Giiiiina-wiiiiina,' he tried.

'Yes?' came a grumpy-sounding reply.

'I can't find my orange T-shirt. I've looked through your drawers and everything.'

'You've looked through my drawers?' Gina was at the bottom of the staircase now.

'Quick!' Niffy urged. Menzie hurried to stand beside his brand-new friend and they shut the door, leaving it open just enough to see.

'Why are you in my room? Why are you looking through my drawers?' Gina was shouting. She began to run up the stairs, two at a time. 'I've told you like a gazillion times not to go into my room, Menzie!' She reached the wide hallway at the top of the staircase. 'Menzie? Menzie! If you're still in there I'm gonna—'

Gina rushed towards the door of her bedroom, turned the handle and ran with an astonishing smack straight into the booby-trapped door.

For a moment she was too surprised to say anything. Then, rubbing her bumped forehead, she yelled out: 'OWWWWW! Menzie, when I find you, I am going to kill you!'

This caused both Niffy and Menzie to shoot out of their hiding place and race down the stairs. They didn't stop running until they were out on the terrace, where Min and Amy were gliding along in the heated pool and Lorelei was sunning herself in the mild sunshine.

'Menzie? Have you and Gina been fighting?' Lorelei wanted to know.

'Not exactly . . .' Menzie said.

'Sorry . . . it's kind of my fault,' Niffy admitted. 'I was showing Menzie how to do this trick and Gina sort of *walked straight into it.*' These words made both Menzie and Niffy laugh.

'I suppose you think you're really, really funny,' Gina stormed, as she walked through the huge glass door and out onto the terrace. She was holding a flannel to her forehead. 'Yeah, I just can't wait to go to the party with some great lump on my head. Fantastic! Fabulous look. Thanks a lot, Niffy.'

'Sorry . . . I didn't mean to hurt you.'

'No, you just wanted me to walk into my own door. I suppose you think doors are made of rubber. Or maybe you think my head's made of rubber.'

'Gina . . . let's not make this out to be a big deal. Niffy's our guest and I think she was just trying to keep Menzie entertained . . . Which is very nice of you, Niffy.'

Now Niffy felt totally embarrassed. She had played a mean trick on her friend and now she had Lorelei trying to be nice about it.

'Are you girls going to start getting ready soon?' Lorelei wanted to know. 'If I'm going to drive you over there, we'll need to leave by four-thirty, because I think there might be traffic.'

'We do not want to get there early,' Gina warned.

'No, I totally understand. But you don't want to miss out on a whole hour of fun.'

'No!' both Gina and Amy chorused together.

'We need to go and get ready,' Amy said, swimming towards the side of the pool. 'I hope everyone's decided what they're going to wear – on top of their swimsuits, obviously.'

'Well . . .' Min began. 'I like my red sundress with the matching cardigan.'

'I wasn't exactly planning on parties when I did my packing,' Niffy admitted.

'I'm sure Gina will be totally happy to lend you something,' Lorelei added. 'She has a wardrobe about five times as big as it needs to be; surely there has to be something in there that you might like.'

Gina turned to Niffy and glared at her. As if it wasn't bad enough that Niffy had caused her to walk into a door and go to the party with a red head, now her mom was going to make her lend Niffy some of her beautiful clothes!

Lorelei had *no idea*. Niffy was a girl who could shred a pair of tights just by looking at them, who could stain a dress about five seconds after putting it on. She would probably jump into Larson's pool fully dressed!

Whatever Gina lent to her, it either had to be indestructible or completely unwanted.

Niffy looked at Gina slightly helplessly. 'It's OK,' she said. 'I'm really happy to go in my jeans and a T-shirt.'

Gina looked back. 'No,' she said, losing the glare, losing her annoyance completely. 'You know how much fun Amy and I always have when we dress you up.'

'Uh-oh. Who said anything about you and Amy dressing me up?'

Chapter Seventeen

'Please tell me you're ready,' Lorelei shouted up the staircase towards the bedrooms at 4.38 p.m., 'and don't dress too skimpy. It's gotten a lot cooler now that it's clouded over. I hope the Jurgensons heat their pool, or else you are all going to come home with pneumonia. In fact, I might even call them to ask.'

'Mom! Don't be so mom-ish!' Gina shouted down.

'Come on,' Lorelei urged. 'I'm dying to see you all.'

'Me too,' Menzie said, taking up a critical position beside his mother.

Min was the first to hurry down the stairs, eager not to hold her hostess up. In her red sundress with matching red cardigan and red pumps, she looked really cute. Amy had done a nice job of curling Min's below-the-shoulder, black, straight-as-a-die hair, even though Min had insisted that she would be going straight into the pool because it sounded like a fantastic place to hide from strange boys at a party.

'You look lovely,' Lorelei told her. 'I like that you have leggings on too; it might get really cold later. OK, glamour pusses, it really is time to go,' she called up to the others.

'OK . . .' Gina called.

Then out came Amy in a sparkling blue sequinned tunic which she'd bought when she was still flush with Daddy's money. She wore it with white leggings and high-heeled purple sandals, deep purple-blue eye shadow and her hair let loose all over her shoulders. She looked at least seventeen and she loved it.

'Oh my word,' was Lorelei's reaction, but as there was no cleavage and no outrageously short miniskirt with exposed leg, there wasn't much she could complain about. 'Very pretty,' she managed. 'Do you maybe have a jacket you could wear with that, sweetheart? I just promise you the heat of the sun might not last, and I'd hate for you to get cold. Especially if you have wet hair from the pool.'

Amy gave a little shriek at the thought of wetting the hair she'd spent so long straightening to perfection. But she also went off in search of a jacket, thinking that it must be quite nice to have a mom like Lorelei, who cared so much about the little details.

'OK, Gina, let's see you, I won't bite,' Lorelei said to coax her daughter out.

Gina appeared at the top of the stairs in a totally tight, totally strappy minidress with long, long button-up-the-back boots.

Lorelei looked at the clothes for a good long moment. 'Have I seen this outfit before?' she asked.

'I don't know . . . I bought it over here,' Gina answered.

'Well . . . it's very . . .' Lorelei paused; she was searching for the right word. 'Flirty,' she decided on.

'Mom! I really want to wear this.'

'Fine . . . just don't blame me if you get pushed in the pool. And you have to take a jacket. That's a non-negotiable. Now, where is your friend? I hope you've not made her look too . . . flirty as well.'

'Niff!' Gina called.

Rather reluctantly, it seemed, Niffy stepped out of Gina's room. She was unrecognizable.

'Is that *you*?' Menzie said with astonishment.

Niffy wobbled towards the top of the stairs. She was wearing high-heeled black boots, a tiny, tiny black minidress and her short hair had been curled and sprayed into thick ringlets. The most obvious thing about her heavy make-up was the bright red lips.

'Oh my . . .' Lorelei began, almost under her breath.

Niffy wobbled towards the first step.

'Are you totally comfortable going to the party dressed like that?' Lorelei asked, her voice sounding kind.

'Well . . .' Niffy gripped onto the handrail and wobbled down another step. 'I don't feel totally comfortable. Not totally,' she admitted.

'You know what? Why don't you swap the boots for pumps and put on a pair of jeans, or something, under that dress? I just think . . . it's a pool party. You want to be able to walk around, have fun. You don't want to have to sit down all the time because you're frightened to fall in the pool if you get up.'

'Mom! She looks great,' Gina protested.

'No . . . I think that's a good idea,' Niffy said.

'Pumps and leggings, short ones, just below the knee,' Amy advised. 'If you don't have some to lend her, then I do.'

'OK . . . back to my room,' Gina said with a sigh.

'I don't think you're going to get there on time,' Menzie said to Min, pointing at his watch.

'And one more thing,' Lorelei called up the stairs.

'If anyone is wearing anything of mine, could they take it off now, please?'

Finally they were pulling up in Lorelei's swanky car outside the electronic sliding gates of Larson's place.

'Does everyone in California have electric gates, a driveway and a pool?' Niffy had to ask.

'California is a really big state about twice the size of Britain,' Gina answered. 'It's pretty swanky around here, but no . . . everyone does not have gates, or a driveway or a pool.'

'Definitely not,' Lorelei agreed. 'I'll park up here and see you through the gate.'

'You're not going to come in, Mom?' Gina asked, with a look close to fear on her face.

'No, don't worry. But switch your cell on. I'll be here at nine p.m. to take you home. Four and a half hours of pool partying is long enough.'

'Nine p.m.!' Gina moaned.

'These guys are fourteen. I think you're probably going to be completely bored of them by then. Call me at eight-thirty and beg to stay longer if you want to. I'll decide then.'

'OK.'

'I'm sure we'll be fine to come back, maybe even

before then,' Min said. She looked nervous at the thought of partying with so many people she didn't know.

The gate slid open, all four girls said goodbye to Lorelei and stepped up the driveway into the bright welcome of the pool party. Multicoloured signs directed them round the side of the large house, but they could also follow the noise. *Whoops*, splashes and thumping music were all luring them towards the pool in the back garden.

'I feel a bit shy,' Amy admitted.

'Me too,' Gina said, 'and I kinda know most of these people.'

'C'mon, we'll be fine.' Niffy urged them all forward.

As they rounded the corner, Amy, Niffy and Min – who'd all never been to a pool party before – couldn't help uttering: 'Wow!' 'Cool!' and 'Amazing!'

The huge blue pool was full of inflatables, noodles, lilos – and teenagers. All around the edge of the water there were chairs and loungers crammed with fit bodies in trunks, swimsuits and bikinis. A huge food table had been set out under a bright striped awning, and a slightly harassed-looking mom and dad were manning a mighty gas barbecue.

The bright colours, the bright light, the blue sky scattered with clouds – it looked totally dazzling.

'Just like a film set,' Niffy decided.

'Hey, guys!!' Paula was the one who spotted them first. She leaped up from her lounger and rushed towards them. 'You made it!'

'Yeah.'

'OK, you have to come over and meet everybody and then you can go into the "girls only" room in the house and put on your swimsuits.'

'Maybe we could go over to the barbecue and get something to eat first?' Min suggested. 'The thought of meeting a whole load of new people while wearing a swimsuit is just a little scary.'

'Sure,' Paula agreed. 'First off, come and meet Larson and wish him a happy birthday.' She walked back with them towards the sun lounger next to hers. 'Larson!'

Immediately, a tall, tanned boy with incredibly fair hair and bright orange swim shorts stood up. When he grinned his bleached blue eyes and white teeth honestly sparkled.

'Hey,' he said with a friendly shrug. 'Gina, hi. Tell me all about your Scottish friends.'

'This is Luella, but we call her Niffy, then there's Min and this is Amy.'

'Hi. Wow. Welcome. Splash, eat and enjoy.'

'Hi!'

'Happy birthday.'

'Thanks for inviting us.'

'Wow . . . you came all the way from Scotland.' His eyes seemed to catch Amy's as he said this.

'Yeah . . . it's not so far, really,' she replied. 'You just get on a plane and stay on it till you get here.'

'I guess. Grab something to eat, I'm gonna change the music and get the party started!'

So they all walked over to the food. There were all kinds of things set out that the dorm girls had never even seen before. Gina and Larson's mom did some of the 'translating'.

'This is peanut butter fluff pie. No, don't ask what it's made from – just try a slice. You're gonna love it.'

'This is guacamole. This is salsa. Tacos? Right, you just take a shell, fill it up with salad, refried beans or a little chilli, then enjoy.'

There was eating . . . there was chatting to some of Gina's former classmates. Then there was changing in the large white TV room set aside for the girls.

'You look great in that swimsuit,' Gina told Niffy. 'What a fabulous figure.'

'Like an ironing board.' Niffy looked down at herself with less enthusiasm.

'Like a supermodel.'

'Shame about the hair.'

'We dealt with that little problem; it's all over.'

Niffy coloured up at this mention of the waxing intervention. 'I meant on my head,' she said, causing Amy to nearly collapse with laughter. 'It's a shame all your ringlets and tong-work is going to be ruined just as soon as I jump into the pool.'

'Well ... at least your make-up is waterproof,' Gina said.

'*That is a relief.*'

'There's no need to be snippy – you enjoyed having us make you look pretty.'

Niffy didn't say anything else.

In the hour that followed, there were pool games and swimming races which helped everyone to have fun and get to know each other.

Niffy won all the girls' races and ate an extra slice of peanut butter fluff pie as a reward.

Min found Ria, and over peach and cranberry coolers they talked about Ria's sister and the stress of dealing with doctors and hospitals.

It didn't seem to matter if Amy was in the pool

or outside the pool; she kept bumping into Larson.

'Hi, how are you? Great party,' she told him. 'Is this how you celebrate your birthday every year?'

'Yeah!' he grinned. 'Except when it's raining.'

'I can't imagine it ever rains here.'

'Tell me about Scotland. I've had this thing about that country ever since I was small.'

'Do you have Scottish relatives?'

'Nah. Norwegian, way back, but we're talking *way* back.'

'Well ... Scotland ... it's a very green place, very misty, foggy ... not like here at all.'

'We can do fog.'

'Believe me, less mist and fog is good. I'm enjoying every moment of blue sky over here.'

They talked for a few more minutes until Paula came over and, throwing Amy something of a puzzled look, told Larson: 'Hey, Zachy wants you to come over and help him pick out some new music.'

'OK, sure, catch you later, Amy.'

Once they'd gone, Amy suddenly felt very alone. An island marooned in the middle of the party. It looked as if everyone around her was engrossed in the most interesting conversation they'd ever had in their entire life.

She looked all around for her friends, but couldn't see any of them anywhere. That's when she suddenly started to feel very hot. The bright sun was beating right down on her head. All around was white: white paint, white walls, white tiles, which were just throwing the sunshine back at her. She had to get somewhere shady, sit down and have a long, cool drink. This was obviously way too much sunshine for someone who'd grown up in Scotland.

The house looked too far away; she worried that she might stumble or even faint if she had to walk all the way over there, but just behind her was the pool shed, probably where all the loungers and inflatables were kept. If she could just get to that door, get inside, get into the cool darkness, she was sure she could recover.

Amy walked the short distance, pulled open the door and felt immediately relieved by the darkness. It wasn't cool in here; in fact, it felt quite hot and stuffy, but it was soothingly dark. She shut the door behind her, opened her eyes wide and realized she could barely see anything. Her eyes hadn't yet adjusted from the dazzling sunshine outside.

Then the door opened with a blast of light, shut again

and she was standing in the fuzzy brown darkness right beside someone.

'Are you OK?' the someone asked and his voice sounded husky and familiar to Amy. His bare arm brushed against hers.

'Yes,' she whispered, aware that her skin seemed to have suddenly become super-sensitive and she could feel him, feel the warmth he radiated, without even having to touch him. She reached out her hands without even knowing which part of him she was reaching for.

Who was he?

He sounded a little like Larson; he sounded a little like the really good-looking guy in the *Twilight* films. As soon as one of her fingertips had landed on the warm skin of his waist, Amy didn't care who he was any more because their faces were turned to each other and they were kissing.

Oh ... yes.

Amy's eyes were shut and her mouth was hungrily feeling for his. It had been so long since she'd kissed someone. She hadn't realized just how desperate she'd been to be kissed, to be held like this. His bare chest, bare arms, bare belly pressed up against her, his gorgeous face leaning in to kiss hers.

This was heaven.

And they were right here, in the secret darkness of the pool shed while the birthday party carried on right around them.

Now the kissing slowed down. It wasn't quite so hurried and frantic. They were kissing, long and deep. His hands were on her bare back, drawing circles on her skin. She ran her fingers through his silky hair. She opened her eyes and looked at his golden cheek.

It was Larson, she saw with a jolt. It really was him. He was like caramel, like a warm caramel kiss.

His hand felt for the string at the nape of her neck and before she could think about what he was doing, the string was pulled and her bikini top had fallen down. Amy immediately put her hands over her boobs, but much as she wanted to break off the kiss and tell him off, she couldn't. It was too nice, it felt too good.

The door creaked and then opened, and although Paula began saying, 'Oh there you—' she broke off immediately.

'Paula!' Larson exclaimed. He jumped away from Amy, leaving her standing, hands over naked boobs, her bikini top dangling.

'Ohmigod!' Paula cried out, and banged the pool-shed door shut.

'No, wait!' Larson called after her, then he ran out of the shed too.

'Oh, great!' Amy said to herself. 'Just great. This is just totally great.' She pulled up the bikini, tied the bow back in place, made sure everything was tucked in . . . then she smoothed over her hair and rubbed her lips dry.

She had just snogged Paula's boyfriend. And Paula had seen her.

Amy was in the biggest trouble ever.

She would have liked to hide in the shed for as long as possible, but she had a feeling that wasn't going to be possible. Eventually, she would have to go out and face the music, so she might as well get it over with. She had no idea what she was going to say . . . or who she was going to say it to. But she had definitely helped to make Larson's fifteenth birthday one of his more memorable ones . . . that was for sure.

She put her hand on the pool-shed door and pulled it open. Once again, her eyes needed a moment to adjust to the difference in the light. When she could focus, she saw Paula and Larson arguing on the other side of the pool, and every single other head turned in her direction.

'Her top was off!' Paula yelled at the top of her

voice, then she spotted Amy and pointed accusingly at her.

Both Niffy and Min were headed in Amy's direction, looking protective. Gina was standing exactly between Paula and Amy. She kept looking over from one to the other, as if she couldn't decide who to go to first. Then she went over to one of the loungers, retrieved her bag and fished out her mobile.

Amy thought she saw Gina's lips form the words, 'Hi, Mom, we have to go!'

Chapter Eighteen

Amy glanced from Paula and Larson over to Larson's mom and dad. His dad was busy with the barbecue and didn't seem to have noticed that anything unusual was happening. But his mom was holding a server with a helping of salad in midair and watching the argument with her mouth open in a little 'o' of surprise.

Paula was pushing Larson away and she was marching round the pool in Amy's direction. Now Amy felt seriously worried.

'What's happened?' Niffy asked, reaching Amy first.

Amy decided it would be best to be honest, get it all out in the open as quickly as possible. 'Ummmm . . . well, I kissed Paula's boyfriend – I didn't know it was him – and she caught me.'

'You *what*?' Min asked, having got to her side just in time to hear this.

'I kissed her boyfriend. I know. But it was really dark. And he undid my bikini top. Completely cheeky.'

'She's headed this way,' Niffy pointed out.

'She looks like a bull about to charge,' Min added.

'Do you think I should run?' Amy asked.

'Where to?' Niffy wondered.

'You! *You!* How could you?!' Paula shouted out. She was only a few metres away now and closing in.

'Look, we kissed,' Amy began. 'We both did it. It was really dark in there; I didn't even know it was him at first.'

'*What?* Do you expect me to believe that?' Paula's hands were on her hips; her whole face seemed to be screwed up and pushed into Amy's. She was scary. Even her hair seemed to be standing on end with fury.

'Why don't you ask him why he was kissing me? I'm not the one with the girlfriend!'

'*What?*' Paula repeated.

'He's fifteen; it's not like you two are married.'

That did it.

That completely did it.

Paula let out a scream of rage and shoved Amy so hard that she toppled over and fell backwards into the pool.

There was a whoop from the crowd.

Larson's mom let the salad fall from her tongs and splatter over the beautiful buffet table. Some of it even landed on the cherry cheesecake.

'Paula, I think you need to calm down,' Niffy suggested.

'I think you should go. I think you should all go!' Paula exclaimed. Now she looked upset as well as furious.

'Probably a good idea,' Niffy decided.

Amy was swimming to the other side of the pool. She pulled herself out, grabbed for the nearest towel and ran inside the house.

'I think I'll just get our stuff together,' Gina said.

'We'll help,' Min offered.

'She does have a point about your boyfriend,' Niffy told Paula before she too headed towards the house to get dressed. 'He was kissing her just as much as she was kissing him.'

'What were you thinking?!!' Gina had to ask as soon as she caught up with Amy in the girls' changing room.

'Sorry,' Amy said huffily, rubbing at her wet hair with the towel, 'but the next time you're in a pool shed and some gorgeous guy comes in and starts snogging you, why don't you stop to have a long think about it too?

You know . . . we just *kissed*.' She was trying to pull on her leggings, but as she wasn't properly dry yet, they were sticking and dragging.

'Well, we'll have to leave. We'll just have to get dressed and leave. We can meet Mom in the street outside. We can't spoil the party for them.'

No one said anything. They knew Gina was right.

'This is so tragic . . . I didn't even get to try the snickerdoodles. I still don't even know what they are,' Niffy complained.

'Oh, shut up!' was Amy's furious response.

'Cinnamon cookies,' Gina said. 'That's what a snickerdoodle is.'

'Oh . . . I don't really like cinnamon, so I suppose we can go.'

There was a tap at the door.

'If that's Paula,' Gina whispered, 'I'll speak to her myself.'

'Girls, are you OK in there? Is everything OK?'

'It's Larson's mum,' Amy whispered.

Gina rolled her eyes. 'Yeah, we're fine. Really. There's been a bit of a . . . misunderstanding, Mrs Jurgensen. We're going to get dressed and head off home now. But really, it's been a fabulous party . . . Look, we'll come out and see you when we're done in here.'

'OK . . . I don't want you to think you have to go . . . Oh boy, I guess this is embarrassing. Larson's just a kid, messing about. I really hope he hasn't hurt anyone's feelings . . .'

'No, it's fine. Please don't worry,' Amy replied, turning a shade of pink that had nothing to do with the sunshine.

'Jeeeeeeeez,' Gina let out with a sigh. 'How is Paula ever going to get over this?'

'Let's just get out of here,' Amy said. She bundled all her wet things into her bag. 'Everyone else ready?'

'Yes,' Min and Niffy replied together.

As they walked down the corridor, they found Larson's mom waiting for them. Both Amy and Gina had to tell her once again that everything was OK.

'I'm sure it will pass,' Mrs Jurgensen said. 'In a couple of days, everyone will have forgotten all about this.'

'Yeah . . .' Gina said, but she sounded unconvinced.

'Great party,' Niffy said cheerfully. 'Fantastic food. Thank you very much.'

'Do you want to go out the front door? It takes you to the driveway. Are you getting picked up?'

'Yeah . . . don't worry,' Gina replied. 'Look, you guys wait for me by the gate. I'll just go and . . . say goodbye to some people.'

It was nearly ten minutes before Gina appeared at the gate to meet her dorm buddies.

'What's going on?' Amy asked.

'Well . . . Paula's getting her stuff together. She's going to leave too . . . I think Maddison and Ria will leave with her and look after her. She's really upset.'

Amy let out a sigh.

'I think we should get through this gate and walk to the end of the road before they catch up with us,' Min suggested. 'We don't want a big showdown.'

'No,' Amy agreed.

As soon as they'd opened the electric gates and gone through, Gina couldn't help asking again, 'Why *did* you kiss Larson? I mean, why were you even *in* the shed? Couldn't you just have told him to get out?'

'Look, I was in the shed because I suddenly felt that everything was so hot and so bright and I had to get out of it or I thought I was going to melt, or die, or have a heart attack or something!' Amy exclaimed. 'Larson came in, stood right next to me, touched me and then we were kissing. I wasn't sure it was him until we kissed . . . Look, if a very hot guy comes and stands beside you in a shed, when you're all blurry and overheated, don't be surprised if you kiss him. Maybe it's jet lag,' she said finally.

'Jet lag? Jet lag??!' Gina repeated. 'That is just about the lamest thing I ever heard.'

'Is that your mum's car?' Min pointed down the street.

'Yeah, I think so,' Gina replied. 'I don't know what to do, Amy, I don't know how I'm going to explain this to Paula. I don't think she'll ever, ever forgive you.'

Chapter Nineteen

'Niffy? Are you awake?' Min asked in a whisper.

It was early. She'd looked at her watch and knew that it was 6.30 a.m. Californian time, but she'd been awake for ages and couldn't imagine getting back to sleep now.

Niffy made a sort of groan in response.

'Niffy, I think we should get up. I bet Lorelei is already up, and we could find out how we can go and hike in the redwoods today, because that's what I really, really want to do. Before anyone comes up with any other plans.'

'Me too,' Niffy said, sitting up and rubbing the sleep from her eyes. 'I've had enough mall-trawling and pool-partying. Gina was talking about going surfing today ... but if we go for our hike in the morning, maybe we can still surf in the afternoon.'

'Or another day. We still have a few days left,' Min pointed out.

'Yeah,' Niffy agreed.

They got washed and dressed quickly, then tiptoed down the stairs to see if anyone was about yet. For a few moments, they stood in the beautiful white and marble hall, just listening. The faint tapping of someone using a keyboard was just audible.

Gina's first tour of the house had included the beautiful office on the ground floor, overlooking the pool; that's where the tapping seemed to be coming from.

'Shall we go into the office?' Min asked, a little doubtful.

'Yeah, I'm sure if we knock on the door it will be OK. I mean, I know Lorelei's a super-busy, executive type, but she is quite nice. To us, anyway.'

So Niffy went over to the door and knocked.

'Hi there!' a male voice called out.

Niffy and Min looked at each other.

'C'mon in,' the voice insisted.

Niffy pushed open the door and both girls stepped into the room.

There, at a glass table, tapping away at a super-slim, ultra high-tech laptop, was a broad-shouldered man with a blondish-grey tangle of curly hair. He was lightly tanned, with a face which looked quite amazingly like Menzie's.

'Hi, I'm Mick Royce, great to meet you. You must be early birds just like me.' He got up from the table, walked over and shook both of them by the hand.

'I'm Luella but everyone—'

'Calls you Niffy. I've heard.' He turned to Min. 'And you must be Asimina.'

'Min,' Min said with a smile.

'I hope I didn't surprise you. I got back late last night, a day early . . . Are you looking for breakfast? I'm sure I could put something together for you in the kitchen.'

'Well, that would be great. But are you really sure? We're not disturbing you?' Niffy asked.

'No, I was just about to start looking for something to eat myself,' Mick assured them.

'We want to find out about hiking in the redwoods,' Min said, as they followed him down the corridors towards the state-of-the-art kitchen, where Teresa, the maid, was in charge between the hours of 9 a.m. and 6 p.m.

'That's great!' Mick said, turning to smile at Min. 'Not nearly enough of our guests go hiking in the forests. Gina should definitely go more. It's amazing and it's easy to get to. I'll drive you up to the entrance of the Malibu Creek State Park. You can get guides from the rangers and make straight for the redwoods.'

'They're really as easy to get to as that?' Niffy asked.

'Yeah, and they look totally amazing up close. You won't believe how tall and majestic they are.'

'Cool,' Min said. 'Can you take us there after breakfast?'

Mick took a look at his watch. 'I don't think anyone will be handing out maps until 9 a.m. so why don't we aim to be there for then?'

'We've been walking for ages and we've hardly seen any trees at all, let alone redwoods,' Min complained nearly three hours later. She stopped on the path they'd been following through rocky landscape covered with knee-high scrubby grass. 'Are you sure we've been reading the map properly?' she asked.

'Yes!' Niffy insisted. She held out the map for Min to take a look. 'Right, this is where we are; you can see the river down there on the left and the fork in the paths over there.'

'Where are the trees?'

'Well, I thought they'd be in this green patch here with the big R on it. So it should be just ahead of us, if we follow the path to the right, maybe it goes down into a valley past that big rocky bit.'

'OK,' Min said wearily. She reached into the rucksack Mick had given them for their hike and pulled out a bottle of water. 'Do you want some?'

'Yes please. But I'm going to have to find a tree soon. I'm desperate for a wee.'

'Oh, great! Now we have to wee behind trees?'

'I don't think there are any public toilets out here. It's pretty quiet.'

This was true. Amazing though it seemed, they really were in the countryside. A much drier, warmer and somehow bigger countryside than Niffy had ever experienced before, although Min had already said it was a little like being in a game reserve in Africa.

It was ages since they'd even seen another hiker, let alone a car or a toilet.

'It's a big, big country,' Niffy added. 'Like Gina said, the state of California is almost twice the size of Britain.'

'Well, let's head round this hill,' Min decided. 'If we can't see any sign of trees, we might have to think about going back.'

'Never! We can't come all this way and not see a tree!'

'Maybe we could phone the ranger and ask him?'

'Let's look down here first.'

After five minutes of tramping along the path, Min broke the silence with an unexpected question. 'Niffy, did you ever tell Mrs Knebworth what you knew about her . . . um . . . man?'

'No.'

'Do you think that's right?'

'I don't know. I've thought about it a lot. I honestly don't know what to do. I do not want to be the person who tells her. She wouldn't even trust me. I mean, me and Mrs Knebworth? How many run-ins have we had in the past?'

'I know . . . but it's in a newspaper. She'd see the photo, Niffy, she'd see his name and she'd know it was true. She'd be able to ask him about it as well.'

'Well . . . I did sort of do *some*thing about it.'

'Really?' Min stopped walking and turned to look at her friend. 'What?'

'Well, I left the article somewhere . . . I sort of left it somewhere I think she might find it.'

'Where?'

'On my bed, back at the boarding house.'

'You just left it out on your bed?' Min asked, surprised.

'Yeah, it's sort of folded up, so you'd have to be properly nosy to open it and take a look, but I think Mrs Knebworth is just the kind of person who'd make a final sweep of the dorms before the holidays and unfold a scrap of newspaper cutting. Then, at least she's on her own with no girls about when she finds out.'

'That's true ... that's actually quite thoughtful of you.'

'Well, it's not ideal. Nothing about the whole thing is ideal ... but it was the best idea I could come up with.'

'*Oh, wow!*' Min had reached the place in the path, past the rocky hill, which gave the view of the trees first.

Niffy rushed up behind her. 'Amazing!'

Somehow the rocky outcrop had managed to hide the most astonishing grove of redwoods. The majestic trees were further down in a valley, but Min and Niffy hurried along the twisting path to get in amongst them as quickly as possible.

Down on the valley floor, it was cool and dark underneath the trees. The massive trunks shot straight up into the blue sky, dwarfing the two hikers standing underneath them.

'This is so cool, I can't believe Gina and Amy didn't come,' Niffy said.

'They were desperate to surf. And I think Amy wanted to do whatever Gina wanted to do so they could make up about the pool-party incident.'

'True. I'm desperate to surf too, but I wouldn't have missed this. These are amazing. Can you imagine what this place must have been like when it was entirely covered with these trees? It must have been like a prehistoric world. I mean, you can just about imagine a dinosaur coming out at you from between these trees.'

'Don't – don't talk about scary stuff. You know what a vivid imagination I have about scary or squeamish stuff.'

Niffy showed no mercy, she gave a monster-like growl, then a wolfish howl.

'Don't!' Min told her off.

'Look at the size of that trunk. I mean, look at it! I have to walk around it, pace it out, try to get a rough measurement. I mean, even if four people stood in a circle with their arms out, they still wouldn't be able to reach around that tree.' Niffy stepped off the path and onto the forest floor. She headed towards the biggest trunk and began to count out her steps around it. 'Twelve, thirteen, fourteen . . . *Owww!*' She collapsed down onto the ground.

'Nif! What's happened? Has something bitten you?' Min left the path too and stepped gingerly through the knee-high grass and undergrowth towards her friend.

'Owwww! Owwww!' Niffy was moaning.

'What is it?'

'I don't know. I need to take a look . . . Min, I think you should stand back . . .' Niffy said, sounding a little shaky.

'What . . . why?' Min asked, but she was already taking backwards steps. 'It's not a snake, is it?'

'No, it's not a snake. So that's a good thing.'

'What is it?' Min's voice was the one that sounded shaky now.

'It's a splinter.'

'Oh, a splinter; a splinter is no problem. I'll take it out and we'll walk straight back.'

'I think this splinter is a problem. Min, stand back!' Niffy warned. 'I know what you do at the sight of blood and I can't cope with you fainting right now.'

'Look, you need help.'

'Stand back . . . *Ohhhh!*' Niffy groaned.

Min bent down and touched her toes, letting her head dangle between her knees. She wanted to make sure there was plenty of blood circulating round in there before she took a look. She took several sharp breaths in and out. 'OK, I'm fine,' she said to convince herself. 'I'm coming to help you right now.' Then she strode with determination right up to where Niffy was sitting.

'Oh no! Oh no! Oh no!' she gasped when she saw Niffy's foot.

Niffy had undone the straps of her hiking sandal, but she couldn't take the sandal off because a gigantic— *splinter* wasn't the right word: a spear – a stake of wood – had passed right through the bottom of her sandal, the sole of her foot and was now poking through the top, a trickle of blood dripping from the hole.

'It's quite painful,' Niffy said through gritted teeth. Her face had turned completely pale and sweaty.

'We have to get help! We need a doctor . . . we have to get you to hospital. How can you walk anywhere like this?' Min said in a panicky jumble.

Niffy breathed in and out. She wanted to try and remain calm. Very calm, as calm as she could. 'Breathe, Min,' she instructed. 'You are not allowed to faint. OK? Breathe.'

Min closed her eyes; she took in air through her nose and let it out through her mouth. Then she fumbled inside the rucksack and got the phone Mick had given them. He had warned them that the signal might be patchy and to keep checking they were in range.

'Niffy, I don't think we've got a signal down here,' Min said, her voice shaky. 'If I go back up to the top, it might work there.'

'We are miles from anywhere and anyone,' Niffy said, 'but luckily for me, I've got the very clever daughter of two doctors with me, so I have a feeling you're going to know just what to do.'

'I should try the phone first,' Min protested.

'No. You should sort me out first,' Niffy told her.

Min's eyes were still scrunched shut as she blurted out: 'The splinter will have to be removed, there's bug-bite antiseptic spray in my rucksack, so we'll clean it with that, then we'll wrap the foot in a T-shirt or something and . . . hobble as best we can until we find help.'

'OK . . . sounds simple enough,' Niffy said bravely, 'but I don't think I want to take it out. I think you'll have to go down to the foot end and . . . get on with things.'

'Ye-es,' Min agreed, not exactly sounding very confident.

'Look, you'll be fine . . . you just get hold of the sandal, pull it away and the splinter will probably come too.'

'Ye-es . . . I can't believe you're still calling it a splinter – it's like a stake, Niffy.'

'Shhh!' Niffy insisted. 'Let's not exaggerate; I'm going to be fine. You're going to do just fine. Splinter, it is,' she said firmly.

Min realized just how brave Niffy was being, and if part of being brave was calling the stake a splinter, then she would join in for Niffy's sake. And she would be very brave too. She walked down to Niffy's foot. Now that she could see Niffy's face properly, she saw how very white her friend looked.

'Are you sure you don't want me to go and get help?'

Niffy shook her head. 'I could be sitting here for hours. A snake might bite me on the bum. No, I think you'd better pull the bloody thing out and we'll hop along for help together.'

'OK . . . OK . . . OK,' Min said, trying to sound calm. Trying to *be* calm. 'OK . . . put your leg on the ground, so it won't wobble. Hold onto those roots over there, so you can pull against me. If I get hold of the shoe and the splinter, then on the count of three . . . I'll pull this way. Don't you move. You keep completely still.'

'Right. OK. Sounds fine,' Niffy said, but the sweat stains on her red T-shirt were growing larger by the minute.

'Right . . .' Min repeated.

Niffy put her leg down on the ground. Min took hold of the sandal as gently as she could, but even that made Niffy groan with pain. The wooden stake was evil and jagged-looking. Min absolutely knew it was going to hurt as much coming out as it had hurt going in. Maybe even more.

Niffy, lying back, gripping her hands tightly around the tree roots, looked even whiter than before.

'Are you sure?' Min asked.

'Just get on with it!' Niffy snapped.

Min jerked the sandal away hard, very hard.

The cry that Niffy made shot up into the treetops and seemed to reverberate all around the forest.

'OK . . . OK . . . OK . . .' Min was whispering to herself. 'Breathe, stay calm, breathe, stay calm.' She opened her eyes. The sandal, with the stake poking right through it, was in her hand. The stake was covered in blood and bits of things which Min knew she couldn't look at or even think about.

Niffy had collapsed back against the ground and looked very frail and fragile.

'Nif! Nif are you OK?' Min asked urgently.

'Oh *God*, that hurt!' came the angry-sounding reply. 'That really, really, *really* hurt.'

'You were very brave,' Min said, realizing that her own hands were shaking.

'You were very brave too,' Niffy added.

'How does the foot feel?' Min asked, peering over to take a look.

The hole right through Niffy's foot wasn't even bleeding much, but it looked messy and brown with dirt now that the stake had been removed.

'It feels numb, thank goodness. We'd better wrap it up with whatever's in your rucksack and get moving before I start to throb.'

Min began tugging the stake out of Niffy's sandal, so she could put the shoe back on.

'And don't throw that away!' Niffy exclaimed. 'I'm keeping that, gore and all, as a souvenir.'

'A souvenir?' Min asked, holding up the splinter.

'Definitely!'

Min sprayed Niffy's foot all over with the bite solution and eased it into one of the clean, spare socks she'd packed into the rucksack, then she gently put the sandal back on and helped Niffy to her feet.

'Can you put any weight on it?'

'I can put weight on the heel, so I'll be able to hobble along like that.'

'We'll probably meet someone really soon who can go and get help,' Min said, trying to be encouraging.

'Well, I really hope we don't meet anyone for a few more minutes.'

'Why not?'

'Because you know that wee I needed? You're going to have to give me a hand.'

'Niffy, please tell me you're joking?'

'Definitely not joking.'

Chapter Twenty

'So tell just once again how the stake ended up in your foot?' Menzie asked Niffy, his eyes wide with admiration as he held up the grisly stick for close examination. 'What is *that*?' he added.

Niffy leaned over from her sun lounger, heavily bandaged foot out in front of her, and took a look. 'It's flesh, it's what's just under your skin,' she told him matter-of-factly.

'Euwwwww, gross.'

'I was just walking around the tree, because I wanted to work out how wide it was, and *bang!* I stepped on this thing and it went right through my sandal and my foot.'

'Wow! Did it hurt?'

'You bet it hurt, but do you know what hurt even more?'

Menzie shook his head.

'When I got Min to pull it out. That hurt like three times as much and it felt in slow motion too. Then we had to walk for about half an hour until we found this hiker. He had a mobile with a signal, so then the ranger picked us up in his jeep. Your dad took us from the park to that amazing hospital . . . Oh my, that was like the dream hospital; apparently your mum and my travel insurance company argued all afternoon about me being sent there, but anyway, after that . . . things got a bit hazy until I woke up and they fed me dream food, for a hospital, and this morning, they let me come home, but there's hardly any chance I'm going to be able to go surfing,' she added sadly.

'Is that where Gina and Amy have gone already?'

'Yeah . . .'

'And what about Min?'

'I don't exactly know about Min. She's brought her microscope out here with her and she said something about going out to look for specimens.'

'Cool! But what about us? What are we going to do? Please tell me you can think of something fun for us to do because it is sooo boring round here.'

'I agree.' Niffy let out a sigh. 'I can't believe I've

been flown all the way to California – *California* – and I'm not going to be able to surf. I don't even want to go to the beach now because I'll be so jealous I'll probably run into the water, foot bandage and everything.'

This made Menzie laugh.

'Why aren't you at the beach with them?' Niffy wondered.

Menzie shrugged. 'I thought you might like someone to hang out with.'

'That's really nice of you. I'll have to think of some really, really good pranks to make it up to you. While I'm thinking . . . you know that fountain in the courtyard at the front of the house? Have you ever put bubble bath in it?'

'What's bubble bath?'

'Well . . . shower gel. Shower gel would probably do. You need something really foamy. Then all the rushing water really makes it foam.'

Menzie's eyes were lighting up. 'What about the stuff Teresa uses to wash the dishes? That's really foamy.'

'Yes! Fantastic! And there aren't any fish in the fountain, are there?'

Menzie shook his head.

* * *

Gina and Amy were stretched out on thick beach towels on the sand. Amy looked out through her sunglasses at the surfboards lying at their feet, still glittering and wet.

'This is sooo cool. We are surfing. In March! How can you bear to come to Edinburgh every term? How can you bear it?'

'I grew up here,' Gina told her. 'Believe it or not, it can get a little boring.'

'Never!' Amy exclaimed.

'Yeah! For me, Edinburgh is quite exciting and different.'

'Can we swap lives then?' Amy asked.

'I think we might have a problem swapping friends,' Gina pointed out. 'None of my friends want to be friends with you right now.'

Amy let out a sigh. 'I need to do something about that, don't I?'

Gina nodded.

'But I don't know what's best.'

'Paula and Larson broke up,' Gina told her.

'Big surprise there.'

'You shouldn't have made out with Paula's boyfriend.'

'Paula's boyfriend shouldn't have made out with me.'

'You're both in the wrong. You'll have to find a way of saying sorry to her.'

'I just really, really wanted to be kissed. Don't you miss kissing? Aren't you just desperate to see Callum again when we get back? I mean, it's been so long since I kissed anyone. Months and months.'

Gina laughed. 'Yeah, I'm looking forward to kissing Callum again. He's a totally great kisser,' she admitted.

'So was Larson. Dangerously good.'

'But what about Paula?!'

'Am I going to see her again before we leave?' Amy wanted to know.

'I don't know yet; I don't know if she wants to see you. What's the date today?'

'It's Thursday the fourteenth. We leave on Saturday,' Amy said sadly.

'Thursday the fourteenth? I think that's the day Mom said she and Mick had some special client coming to the house for a meeting.' Gina sat up and frowned. 'I'm sure it was today. But she didn't say anything about it when we left. I mean, Niffy and Menzie are there! They might not know about it, they

151

might cause some sort of disaster . . . my mom will totally freak.'

'Calm down, calm right down, you've forgotten about Min,' Amy said. 'The very calming, sensible Min is around. So everything will be just fine.'

Chapter Twenty-one

'I've had really mixed success with door bombs,' Niffy was telling Menzie.

'Door bombs? What is a door bomb?'

'Something you put above a door, so that when someone opens it, it hopefully explodes all over them. But the problem is, if you put it on top of the door, you can't predict where it's going to fall, also people usually see it before they open the door.'

'Wow!'

'I've been thinking for a while about how to attach a long string to a door so I can hide the bomb out of sight. Then when the door is opened, the string is pulled and the bomb gets yanked with a real pendulum effect either into the door or into the person. Now that would be much, much better.'

'Double wow! I have string, we could get started. What do we make the bombs out of?'

'Do you have any balloons?'

'Yeah . . . I think so.'

'Fantastic. Then we just need flour and water.'

'This is the best. You are totally cool, Niffy.'

'Thank you,' Niffy replied, almost a little shyly. 'Where are your parents, by the way? We don't exactly want them to know too much about all this.'

'Both in their office, working. Don't worry about them; we probably won't see them for hours.'

'OK, just pass up the drawing pin . . . right . . . I'll just push that in. Then we'll stretch the string right out and tuck this in over here.'

'Are you sure you're OK?' Menzie asked his brand-new best friend ever.

Niffy was standing with her good foot on a chair, her other foot held up at an angle so she didn't put weight on it by mistake. She was reaching right up to the top of the big white glass and wood front door and wobbling slightly as she pushed in the pin. Now, the large white balloon – filled almost to bursting with flour they'd managed to pinch from the kitchen – was tucked high up on a corner display shelf.

'Brilliant,' Niffy whispered. 'Now, very, very carefully open the door and we'll set one up on the other side.'

With more precarious chair-balancing and pinning, Niffy managed to find somewhere to store the wibbly water-filled balloon. It wasn't as well-hidden as she would have liked, and even the string looked a bit obvious and dangling ... but if someone wasn't looking for it, if someone got a little distraction just before they opened the front door, they might still fall for it.

'OK,' Niffy said, sidling herself very carefully in through the small gap left by the open door, 'shut the door gently, gently, very gently. If you feel any pull on the strings, then just stop right there.'

Menzie was able to close the door to almost-shut.

'Excellent,' Niffy told him.

'Now what?'

'Now we just pick somewhere good to wait and see what Amy and your sister make of our little hello.'

'What if Mom and Dad get to the door first?'

'Ermm ...' Niffy didn't seem to have thought about this. 'We'll see them. We'll warn them. OK?'

'So where do we wait?'

'Where's the place with the best view of the front door?'

Menzie thought hard. 'We could hide in the garden.'

'Not a bad idea.'

* * *

155

As Gina and Amy walked along the street towards Gina's family home, Amy was the first to notice the shiny black convertible pulling up.

'Isn't that your gate the car's stopped at?'

'Yeah,' Gina said, tossing her sea-sprayed hair back over her shoulders. She and Amy were a whole shade blonder and browner after their morning at the beach.

'Which one of your parents owns that one?'

'Neither. That must be the client I told you about. The big important Mr Business.'

'Oh, right. Do you think he'll mind if we go in the gate at the same time as him?'

'No, I'm sure it will be fine.'

'Hi there, are you here to see the Winkelmann-Royces?' Gina waved to the man in the car and hurried over to him.

'Oh, hi, you must be Lorelei's daughter. Gina? Is that right?'

'Yeah. This is my friend Amy. Shall I open the gate for you, save you getting out and having to ring?'

'Thanks.'

As the electric gates slid apart, Gina and Amy walked ahead of the car.

Their mouths fell open at the sight of the waterfall

fountain. A huge pile of white foam was overflowing from the bottom of the elegant water feature. The foam which had already spilled out was collecting in a great marshmallowy mountain. More and more foam was gathering, and there didn't seem to be any sign of it stopping.

'It's Gina and Amy!' Menzie hissed, smacking Niffy on the leg to rouse her from the little doze she'd drifted into behind the bush they'd so carefully chosen.

'Excellent,' Niffy replied, sitting up immediately.

'There's a car behind them. Some guy in a convertible.'

'Let's not worry about him. Gina and Amy are definitely going to get to the door first, so we'll be able to see if the N and M bomb pendulums actually work. Nothing might happen. They might just flop down on their string and just dangle there.'

Menzie was looking worried. He was looking as if he might like the balloon bombs to do just that.

'Don't get all scaredy-cat on me,' Niffy whispered.

'Are you sure?'

'C'mon, it will be hilarious.'

Both of them peered through the leaves of the bush to see what would happen next.

Within moments, Gina was at the front door. She took

hold of the handle and pushed it open. The balloon filled with water thudded down, walloping her on the back and exploding in a high-powered gush of water.

Gina's scream was mingled with the scream of someone else . . . someone Niffy and Menzie couldn't see yet, but Menzie had an idea.

'Uh-oh, I think that's my mom.'

'Uh-oh,' Niffy agreed.

Both Amy and the man in the convertible hurried to the front door at the sound of the screams, and Niffy and Menzie had a feeling that they should probably do the same.

'I think we'd better go and take a look at the damage,' Niffy murmured.

As Niffy and Menzie approached, they saw that both the flour and the water balloons had exploded. There was a white cloud of dust all over the floor and, worst luck, over the very smartly dressed Lorelei. Niffy could just make out Gina's mom's grey silk blouse, pencil skirt and high heels under the flour attack. Even Lorelei's face was covered; they could just see red-stained flour where her lips were.

Convertible Man had rushed up but was now standing by helplessly as he didn't seem to know what to do.

Amy was the first to spot Niffy and Menzie approaching, and she wheeled around to glare at them furiously. Obviously this situation was so serious she didn't even want to accuse them of anything in case she got them into more trouble than they could ever have bargained for.

Gina, soaking wet, with flour sticking to her dripping clothes and hair, also heard Niffy and Menzie arrive on the scene. She turned, saw them and began to yell in fury. She shouted so loudly that everyone else froze. Niffy had the feeling that her ears were vibrating – the yelling was so loud.

'Niffy, this was you! This was completely you! You've covered me in water, you've covered my mom in flour. She has an important guest. How could you have picked today? Every time you do one of these things, everyone just gets completely upset and hurt. You're a guest! Don't you get it?! Don't any of you get it? Amy, you kiss my best friend's boyfriend; Niffy, you ruin my mom's meeting—'

Right on cue, the electric gate slid open and they all turned to watch as a completely bedraggled Min walked in. She was covered almost up to her waist in brown mud, but she had an excited smile right across her face.

'Bugs!' she yelled. 'Amazing bugs!'

'You're all nuts!' Gina shouted. 'You're all completely nuts. You're the worst guests I've ever had. I wish you would just go home and leave me alone!'

And with that, she ran from the doorway, through the hall and up the stairs towards her bedroom.

Convertible Man managed his first words: 'Hi, Lorelei, looks like I've picked a bad moment to show up. Can I get you a towel or something?'

'No, Will, just wait there for a minute,' Lorelei said, sounding just as calm and controlled as she always did. 'I'll get . . . freshened up.' Then she turned on her heel, skidded dangerously in the wet and floury mess on the marble, but managed to right herself and carry on carefully.

As soon as she had crossed the hallway, Menzie couldn't help letting out a snigger. 'She nearly fell,' he whispered. 'Thank goodness you're here,' he told Convertible Man, 'otherwise we would all be like *dead*.'

'Happy to oblige,' Will, as they now knew his name was, replied. Then he began to snigger quietly too. He put his hand over his mouth to cover up. 'What *was* that?' he asked, when he'd got back in control.

'One balloon filled with water, one balloon filled

with flour. One fixed with a drawing pin to each side of the door and hidden out of sight. I've been working on it for a while,' Niffy told him, a little proudly.

But by this time, Min had made it up to the party at the doorway. 'I think I've made a discovery,' she said, her face beaming with happiness. 'I honestly don't think anyone's seen these before.' She opened her hand to reveal a small collecting bottle with several vile-looking cockroach-type things.

'*Urgh!* I don't think anyone wants to see them, either,' was Amy's response. 'Look, the only thing we should be thinking of right now is how to clean up this mess, and how to make it up to Lorelei and Gina.'

'Oh, my goodness, what happened?!' Min asked, spotting the disaster.

Amy sighed. 'What happened? Menzie met Niffy.'

Chapter Twenty-two

'Do you get the feeling we've been banished?' Niffy asked Amy.

'No bloody wonder,' Amy snapped. 'They'll probably throw a tent into the garden and get us to camp out here until it's time to catch our plane.'

Niffy, Amy and Min had all been sent to the pool terrace by Lorelei. They'd expected her to appear a few minutes later to give them a lecture about hurting Gina's feelings. But instead, twenty minutes had passed and no one had appeared at all, then Teresa had come through the glass doors with a tray of tea and biscuits.

Even when the tea was drunk and all the biscuits eaten, still no one came out to see them.

'We are in deep, deep trouble,' Niffy said morosely.

'Do you think I should maybe go inside and try to see Gina?' Amy wondered.

'I could really do with a shower,' Min added. Niffy and Amy turned to look at her. Somehow, they'd not got round to asking Min how she'd managed to get so filthy.

'So what happened exactly?' Amy asked first.

'I was scrambling after one of my bugs when I slithered down into this really deep ditch. I know it seems so dry out here, but this place was so muddy it was quite hard to get out,' Min added. 'But I managed and I got my little bugs as well.' She held up the glass bottle again.

'Please put that away,' Amy urged. 'It's making my skin crawl.'

'Do you think Menzie's getting told off?' Niffy asked, worried for her new friend.

'No,' Amy decided. 'He's probably in the kitchen eating biscuits with Teresa.'

'How are we going to make this up to Gina and Lorelei?' Niffy wondered.

'Maybe you should have thought of that before you set the big joke up. Did anyone even laugh for one minute? Did anyone actually get any fun out of it? You big idiot,' Amy added.

'Will and Menzie ... I saw them laughing ... well ... a bit,' Niffy admitted.

'What time is it in Britain?' Amy asked Min.

Min checked her watch before deciding it was 8 a.m.

'I think I'm going to go inside, get my phone and call Dad,' Amy said.

'You can't tell him about this!' Niffy protested. 'It will probably all blow over.'

'Here's hoping,' Amy said, but she slid off her chair and disappeared in through the terrace doors.

Niffy picked up the teapot and drained out the last trickle. 'Let's hope her dad has some good ideas,' she said.

Chapter Twenty-three

Gina lay on her bed and stared at the wall. Her hair was still wet and there was a smattering of soggy flour over her shorts and her legs.

She had no idea how her mother had managed to stay so calm when the flour bomb had exploded. It must have been because that guy was there. He must be very important.

She thought about her friends and felt a little sorry for what she'd said. She'd called them the worst guests ever . . . and poor Min, all she'd done was go for a walk and fall into some mud. She'd needed some sympathy and attention.

And Niffy . . . she'd been lying with her foot in the air all morning; she'd probably got so bored listening to Menzie that she'd had to create some fun for them.

And Amy . . .

Well . . . hadn't Amy explained herself as best she

could? And really, wasn't it just as much Larson's fault as Amy's?

It was just difficult, having two sets of friends who had now fallen out with each other.

There was a gentle tap on the door.

Gina didn't say anything for a moment. She had a feeling it would be her mom, and she didn't know if she was quite ready to face her just yet. The long talk . . . the advice to go down and face her friends, who were probably all sulking and talking about her.

But then the knock came again, this time with the question, 'Gina, please can I come in?'

It was Amy.

Gina sat up, flicked her wet and gooey hair behind her shoulders and replied grudgingly, 'I suppose so.'

Amy opened the door slowly, closed it behind her, then walked in and even dared to sit herself on the end of Gina's bed.

'I'm sorry,' she said straight away. 'I'm sorry that I ever went anywhere near the pool shed, let alone Paula's boyfriend. I'm sorry that we left Niffy here alone to get into trouble, I'm sorry Min went bug-hunting. I'm sorry your mum got flour-bombed right in front of a very important client, I'm sorry, I'm sorry, I'm really sorry.'

'Flour-bombed!' Gina repeated, and suddenly neither

of them could help it, they were doubled over making helpless little squeals of laughter.

'Her lips . . .' Gina was trying to say. 'Her lips . . .'

'They were just pink stains . . .'

'All over . . . a direct hit,' Gina managed to get out in between squeaks.

'You didn't see . . . you'd left, but when she turned . . .' Amy burst into giggles again. 'She skidded.'

'She fell?' Gina couldn't contain herself at the thought.

'No . . . but nearly, very nearly.'

'OMG, we are dead. We are so dead.'

'I've been talking to my dad,' Amy began.

'You've not told him about all this?'

'Well, not exactly, just a bit. I've said there have been a few moments, and I wanted to know if I could take everyone out to dinner to say sorry.'

'No, Amy. That's really kind of you, but you don't have to.'

'But listen,' Amy went on. 'You know my dad; he's a nightclub boss, he used to be a clubber and a bouncer, he knows loads of really cool people . . . so I asked him where we could go in LA. And he's come up with this amazing idea.'

'Really?' Gina was starting to look excited now.

'Yeah, well, he has this old friend from his DJ days in Tokyo, Wong-Kei, nicknamed Wonky – colourful life, my dad leads – and this guy came to LA . . .'

'Oh my!' Gina's eyes were widening.

'What?'

'I have a feeling I know what you're going to say next.'

'This guy runs a sushi restaurant?'

Gina nodded, eyes even wider.

'Have you heard of it?'

'Wonky's Sushi Bar in West Hollywood. It's like the coolest place. Every single celebrity has dinner there. It's impossible to get into . . .'

'Unless Wonky was a friend of your dad's back in the good old Tokyo days, I guess . . . I have a table for ten for tonight, Dad's credit card and the promise that he'll be paying "mates' rates".'

'A table for ten?' Gina gasped. 'At Wonky's? Are you for real?'

'Yeah, they've probably had to tell Britney Spears to go somewhere else tonight,' Amy joked.

'A table for ten? Who were you thinking of?'

'Well, obviously, the three of us – *the worst guests in the whole world.*'

'Sorry,' Gina interrupted. 'I was a little upset.'

'No wonder. Don't worry, I punched Niffy and stomped hard on her sore foot. No, not really. But I should. Then you and your family, Menzie included, but he has to sit very far away from Niffy, otherwise who knows what they might do ... Blow up the miso soup?'

'And the three extra places? Are you going to invite Paula, Ria and Maddison?'

'Of course, if they'll come.'

'That's really nice of you.'

'I'm sorry about what's happened ... we've only got two more days, can we try and make the most of them?'

'Of course.'

Amy reached out her arms and gave Gina a quick hug.

'A table for ten at Wonky's?' Gina repeated in disbelief. 'Wait till I tell Mom ... wait till I tell Mick ... wait till I tell the girls!'

'Do you think Paula will come?' Amy wondered.

'I think this could be the best kiss-and-make-up present of all time.'

'Kiss? Please don't mention kissing. Don't mention anything to do with kissing.'

Chapter Twenty-four

'Can I park your car, ma'am?'

'Thank you.' Lorelei handed the valet her keys. 'Here we are, guys, bail out,' she told everyone in the back seat. 'I think Mick and the others aren't far behind us.'

Menzie might have been the first to say 'Wow!'

But Amy, Niffy and Min were already thinking it. This place was swanky: much swankier than any restaurant any of them had been to before, even Amy.

A shiny, black awning led from the pavement to the door. The large, brightly lit glass windows on either side showed a golden-coloured place hung with huge ceiling lamps and packed with diners.

Amy climbed out of the car, smoothing down her specially dressed hair, pressing her freshly lipsticked lips together, wobbling on unfamiliar heels and tugging down the dress which had ridden up too high in the car.

'And smile!' Lorelei instructed. 'No need to be nervous, it's just West Hollywood ... and OMG I've just spotted Kirsten Dunst sitting right there at the window!'

'No need to be nervous!' Amy repeated.

The door was held open for them by another member of the immaculately dressed staff and then they were facing the reservations girl. She looked incredibly serious. She had on those headphones with a little mouthpiece and she was tapping intensely at a computer.

'Hi,' Amy began, a little anxiously.

'Hello?' The girl made it a question, not exactly a welcome.

'I believe there should be a reservation for ten under the name McCorquodale.'

'Mc-what?' the girl asked. 'For ten? I don't think so.'

'Let me spell the name out for you,' Amy offered, just about hyperventilating at the thought of them all being turned away.

As soon as the girl had tapped Amy's surname into the computer, she began to look much more friendly.

'Ah, the McCorquodale party, of course! You're Mr Wong-Kei's special guests tonight.'

'Right . . .' Amy confirmed, a little shyly. 'Five of us are here and the other five will be here in a few minutes.'

'Let me call on Sean, he'll take you to your table and look after you tonight.'

Sean appeared in a twinkling, all shiny shoes, shiny hair and shiny white smile. He bowed in front of them and assured them he would look after their every need, their every 'passing whim'.

'A bit over the top,' Niffy whispered to Min.

'Shhh.' Min dug Niffy in the ribs.

They followed Sean to the huge round table which had been set out for them in what felt like the very centre of the restaurant.

'It's the see-and-be-seen table,' Lorelei said to Amy. 'Mr Wong-Kei must really like your dad. Someone important has been moved to get us this table tonight.'

'This is making me nervous,' Amy confessed. 'I don't even know what the man looks like.'

'Oh, don't worry, I do. I've seen him on TV.'

'That's not helping,' Amy told her.

'You'll be fine,' Lorelei said, placing a hand on her

back. And even though Amy had a dad she really, really loved, she couldn't help thinking, once again, with a little pang, that it would be nice to have a mom like Lorelei too.

As soon as they'd taken their seats and each been handed the menu with a Sean flourish, Mick, Gina and her three Californian school friends arrived.

'Hi! Isn't this place *amazing*!' Gina gushed. 'Amy, how will we ever thank you?'

'My dad. It's really him, not me.'

Ria, Maddison and Paula all said an equally cheerful hello. Then Paula's eyes found Amy's and her smile became a little more forced.

'Hello,' Amy said, directly to Paula. 'I'm sorry about what happened. And I'm really glad you could come.'

'Erm . . . thanks. Gina wanted me to come . . . it was cute of you to invite me . . . *considering*.'

'I hope you enjoy the meal . . . *considering*.'

'I'll try,' Paula said, and took a seat a good few places from Amy. She looked as if she wasn't ready to be Amy's new best friend any time soon. But at least the full-on fight was over and Amy had said sorry. It was a start.

'Who's ready for green tea?' Gina asked, desperate to move Amy and Paula on from their awkwardness.

Sean was soon back, recommending special Japanese teas and lychee smoothies. He took extra time to talk through the menu with everyone who'd never eaten Japanese before – Min, Maddison and Menzie – and with the one person who was deeply suspicious of the menu and didn't think she'd be able to find anything she liked: Niffy.

'Tempura,' Sean decided. 'If you don't want your fish raw, then try our light-as-fluff, taste-of-heaven tempura batter.'

When it was Mick's turn for Sean's special attention, he asked, 'So apart from Kirsten at the window, is anyone else in tonight that we can take a peek at?'

For a moment, Sean paused, then he smiled, put his finger up to his lips and whispered, 'You promise you'll be very discreet?'

Everyone nodded.

'Do not look now. Do not. Two tables along, Matt Damon. Then Will Smith and his family are having a party in one of our private dining rooms.'

'Who's Matt Damon?' Menzie wanted to know.

'*Shhh!*' from Gina.

Tea and smoothies, delicate little starters and then

big platters of raw fish and tempura dishes, vegetables and little bowls of soup all began to pile up on the table.

It was fun.

Everyone shared out what they had, offered it to others and tasted as many weird and wonderful things as possible.

Even Niffy decided to give a slice of raw salmon a go.

'Just a dab of wasabi,' Mick urged her. 'It's like English mustard, so you'll feel at home.'

'Not too bad . . .' Niffy decided once she'd swallowed her mouthful. 'Reminds me of the time we had this big party of guests, Mum completely misjudged the timings and served the fish quite like that. A lot of mayo was eaten at that meal, I can tell you.'

Sean suddenly appeared to tell them that: 'Mr Wong-Kei himself is headed your way, you lucky people.'

Everyone looked up and Amy began to blush with nerves. A small, neat Japanese man dressed head-to-toe in black, his hair in spikes was walking towards the table, although he kept stopping to smile and offer little bows to other diners as they turned and recognized him.

'My very warmest welcome to the McCorquodale

party,' he said, as he arrived at their table. 'Which one of you charming girls is Amy?'

Amy raised her hand and blushed a bit more.

Mr Wong-Kei came over to stand next to her. 'Oh my goodness,' he began, 'you are so much better-looking than your father.' This made everyone laugh. 'Gary and I are very old friends. We haven't seen each other for a long time now, but whenever we meet, we have a fantastic time. I hope you are enjoying your meal?'

Everyone nodded and told him 'yes' with enthusiasm.

'It's an amazing place, fantastic food, I'm going to come back as often as I can,' Lorelei told him.

'Mr Wonky?' Menzie piped up.

'Mr Wong-Kei,' Mick corrected him gently.

'Oh, don't worry, it says "Wonky" above the door.'

'Mr Wonky,' Menzie repeated, 'could you take me to meet Will Smith?'

There were laughs and protests from Menzie's parents at this. But Mr Wong-Kei just smiled, beckoned with his finger to Menzie and said, 'Follow me; maybe we can just visit for a quick minute.'

'Wow!' Min said, as Menzie hurried off with Mr Wong-Kei. 'This is cool. This is the coolest place I've ever been to.'

'Agreed.'

'Totally.'

'Yes!'

Once the excitement of meeting the restaurant owner was over, they turned back to their food, began to eat again and Mick, wanting to be friendly, asked, 'Min, is it true you've found some sort of unusual insect?'

'Yes!' Min replied, then she rummaged in her little handbag and brought out the slim glass test tube with the stopper on the end. Only one of her insects was in there, but she held it up proudly.

Although Mick looked intrigued, Lorelei immediately hissed, 'Min – not in a restaurant!'

This startled Min so much that, as she fumbled to hurry the test tube back into her handbag, she dropped it. It fell onto the black marble floor and smashed. With a gasp, Min bent down and began to scramble for the cockroach.

Already Sean was approaching. 'Did I hear the sound of breaking glass?' he asked. 'I'll go and get a brush, please, leave that to me.'

'Thanks,' Min said, as she scooped glass gently with her hand, looking for her insect as subtly as she could.

'Over there,' Niffy whispered, pointing.

Just for a moment, Min caught a glimpse of her bug as it scurried under their table.

'Oh no!' She swiped at the area under Lorelei's shoe, but the bug was too quick and scampered out from under Lorelei's chair towards the table behind her.

'Did you catch it?' Lorelei asked.

Min, still under the table, wailed, 'No!'

She was worried that her specimen blue roach was going to be trampled underfoot. Lorelei was much more concerned that they were about to be sued for bringing roaches into one of the most famous restaurants in town.

Gina's mom stood up, looked carefully at the floor, then walked quickly between the two tables behind her chair. She swooped down, scrabbled for a moment, then came up, a pleased expression on her face.

'Sorry, dropped an earring,' she explained to the surprised diners looking at her from the other tables.

Lorelei's gaze seemed to catch on one of the men at the left-hand table. She looked away, then looked back and stared at him.

'Lorelei?' the man asked.

When she nodded slowly, he added, 'I thought it was you . . . I didn't want to disturb your meal. I just got into town . . .'

'What's going on?' Amy whispered to Gina.

Gina also couldn't take her eyes from the man. He looked tall, even though he was sitting down. He was very smartly dressed in a suit and tie; his short, dark hair was run through with grey. She was looking at him in profile and there was something about his jaw and nose which she recognized: mainly from photos.

'I think . . .' she began in a whisper to Amy. 'I think that man is my father.'

Chapter Twenty-five

'Are you sure you want to do this? Are you totally sure? You can back out at any time. You can just call me, I will be nearby and I will come and get you.'

Gina looked over at her mom in the driver's seat and smiled. 'I'm sure,' she replied. 'Everyone I know has given me more advice than you could believe! I mean, Amy kept me up till two in the morning talking about it. I'm going to be fine. You seem a lot more nervous than me.'

'Well . . . I guess I am. We split up when you were two. You haven't seen him since you were seven. I've hardly heard from him in years, which has been fine with me . . . but maybe it's good for you to know a bit more about him.'

For about the one hundredth time that day, Gina asked her mom, 'Can you tell me a bit more about him?'

Lorelei sighed but then told Gina, 'He's a nice man. When I think back on it, I was probably a lot more to blame for our marriage falling apart than he was. I was so busy with work, I didn't have time for him and I made no effort to get things back on track when they went wrong.'

'Why did he move so far away?' Gina asked.

'He felt he had to move to the east coast for work . . . and maybe to help himself get over everything that had happened. Once he'd moved, it was much harder for him to play a part in your life. Then when he remarried, he didn't want to spend his vacation time coming over here, and you were too small to travel over there. So we didn't lose touch exactly . . . but the contact became much less frequent.' After a pause, Lorelei added, 'I didn't make it any easier for him to be in touch with you, I know that. I didn't really try. I would probably do things differently now. But I met Mick, we had Menzie and the four of us felt like such a happy family. I didn't want to mess with that.'

'So he might have wanted to stay in touch more, but you didn't really encourage him?' Gina asked.

'I guess not . . . I was so busy, I didn't want the complication. I never offered to fly with you over to Boston; I always made him come here to see you, and I guess that wasn't exactly helpful. I'm sorry,' Lorelei admitted.

'I would have liked to see his home.'

'I guess.'

'Does he have another family?'

'Yes.'

'Yes?! So I have half-brothers and sisters I've never even met?'

'Well, I guess . . .'

Gina found this astonishing. 'Don't you think people should get to know this kind of stuff? I mean, one day I could meet my half-brother and date him by mistake. *Gross*.'

'Gina, please, save some of your questions for him, will you?' Anxious for a change of subject, her mom asked, 'Have you had a good time with your friends?'

'Yeah. The house will be so quiet when they've gone.'

'Yes, but in a good way. No flour bombs, no foaming fountains, no escaping cockroaches.'

'Menzie will be sad.'

'I'll have to keep a close eye on Menzie; I hate to think about the Niffy-inspired jokes we're going to have to deal with over the next few weeks.'

'Yeah, well, except for a hiccup or two, it's been great.'

'So . . . back to school in less than two weeks?'

'I'll miss you guys.'

'We'll miss you too . . . Oh, Gina, here we are. I'll park up. So, I'll take you in, say hello and wait for you nearby. Are you sure that's going to be OK?'

'Yes! Mom, it's weird that you're not at work. You used to be at work like the whole time.'

'Yeah, well apparently this is called a vacation and I'm quite enjoying it,' Lorelei replied with a smile.

Gina listened to the *click, click, click* of her mom's shoes disappear into the distance before she turned to face the slightly familiar stranger sitting opposite her at this cute little diner.

She liked that he'd picked a diner. It was a blue and white place, full of sunshine and probably wholesome salads and fruit shakes.

The kind of place a dad would take his daughter for lunch.

'You must have a lot of questions,' he began.

The man she vaguely recognized from old photographs was wearing an open-necked pink shirt today. He looked smiley and friendly, but a little tired and creased around the eyes.

'Have you got jet lag?' she asked first.

'No. Not much. But I stayed up really late last night. I had a work party, and then I was lying awake . . . worrying about how this would go.'

'Me too,' Gina confided. 'By the way, are you really called Peter? Peter Peterson?'

'Yes, but it's Pieter, with an "i".'

'Oh, that's OK then, Pieter with an "i",' Gina teased.

'It's a traditional Scandinavian thing.'

'How Scandinavian are you?'

'Not very. There are some Swedish ancestors, way back.'

'Gosh. So I'm part-Swedish, part-German, part-Scottish?'

'But all-American.'

They laughed a little, and the waitress brought them menus and took their drinks orders.

'Why don't you tell me about Boston and where you live? And I'd like to know all about your family too.'

'Yeah . . .' Pieter Peterson ran his fingers through his hair a little awkwardly. 'I have three other children . . . you've never met them and this does feel strange, Gina, that I know them very well and I don't know you at all.'

'Do you have any pictures?'

Pieter took his phone out of his pocket, called up the photo album and handed it to her. Gina laid the phone flat on the table so they could see the pictures together.

'This is Milly, my wife, with Stan, our youngest – our boy.'

'How old is he?' Gina asked.

'Nine.'

'Menzie is ten. He's my brother,' Gina explained.

'Well . . . so is Stan . . .' Pieter said gently

Gina flicked up the next picture. Twin girls, both blonde just like her, both looking . . . well . . . just like her sisters might look.

It made Gina gasp. She'd always wanted to have sisters. And here they were.

'This is Elle and this is Eliza. They're eleven.'

'They are so pretty. And they look loads of fun too; look at her smile – that is one cheeky smile!' Gina pointed at Eliza.

This made Pieter laugh. 'You're right, Eliza is quite a handful.'

'Lucky you; you broke up with Mom and me but you got a lovely new family to take our place.'

Pieter put his hands over hers and suddenly looked upset. 'I never wanted to *break up with you*. I'm truly sorry that I let it happen.'

'It's OK,' Gina said quickly, feeling awkward. 'Mom said she didn't really help you to stay in touch. Anyway, I was really small when you left, I don't think I noticed much. I'm not like really scarred or anything.'

This didn't have the soothing effect on Pieter that she'd been hoping for. In fact, he covered his face with his hands and his shoulders shook a little as if he was trying to contain his sobs.

'It's really OK,' she repeated.

'No. It's not. I'm sorry; I should have tried much harder to stay in touch. To keep up to date with you. You should have spent time at my house with the other people in your family. You really should have. It was up to me to make sure that it happened. Lorelei didn't want it and you were too small.'

'Here are your drinks.' The waitress appeared and banged two big fruit smoothies down on the table. This seemed to help Pieter calm down a little.

'Thanks,' he said, his voice almost back to normal.

'What would you like to eat?' the waitress asked.

'Ummm . . .' Gina gave the menu a quick once over. She didn't exactly feel hungry. 'Chef's salad, please,' she decided.

'That would be fine for me too,' Pieter added.

Once the waitress had gone, Gina and her father looked at each other a little helplessly, but smiled.

'I guess we just have to start out from here,' Gina suggested gently. 'In the summer vacation, maybe I could come over to Boston and visit with you all. You know ... if that would be OK, if you'd all like to do that?'

'We'd love that, Gina. I was going to ask you if you'd like to do it. To be honest, my children are desperate to meet their big sister.'

'Really? Pieter ... is it OK if I call you Pieter – it's just, I've called Mick "Dad" for a long time ...'

'Pieter is fine.' But Gina noticed the slightly pained expression which passed over his face.

'Would you have got in touch with us if Mom hadn't seen you in that restaurant?'

'Yes, but I didn't know how to do it: by phone, by letter, by email?'

'You could have asked to be my friend on Facebook?' Gina offered.

'Not after all these years. I didn't know what was going to be best. The trip got closer and closer, then I was here and I still hadn't gotten in touch. So, although I may have spoiled your dinner—'

'No. Not really, the dinner was already completely crazy. I was beginning to wonder what would happen next. The cockroach, then you, then Menzie getting brought back to the table by Will Smith . . . that was a moment.'

'I'm real glad the way it worked out.'

The waitress clanged salad plates down in front of them and gave an insincere: 'Enjoy your meal now.'

'So, you're boarding in Scotland? Your mom's old school. I'd love to hear all about that.'

'Would you?' Gina stuck a fork into the shredded lettuce and carrot in front of her.

'Tell me about your friends first,' Pieter asked. 'What are they like?'

'Well, I have three really good friends at school. First off, there's Amy . . . we have the most in common, including the fact that her mum left when she was small. In fact, she's desperate to know how our meeting goes, because she thinks it will help her decide if she should get in touch with *her* mum or not.'

Chapter Twenty-six

Amy was packing. Scattered across Gina's bed were all the things she still had to fold and find room for in her suitcase.

There were the clothes she'd brought over from Scotland, the few new things she'd picked up in the shops over here, then there were also some chosen items from Gina's 'closet', which Gina had insisted she should take.

Gina was still standing in front of the huge walk-in cupboard, trying to decide if there was anything else Amy could have.

'Stop it!' Amy insisted when Gina held out another summer dress. 'I haven't got room. The seams are already threatening to burst on my bag and I've still got all this to get in.'

The big discussion about Gina's reunion with her dad was still in full swing. Amy was trying to get every possible little detail from Gina, who wasn't tired of talking about this interesting new development yet either.

'How did you feel when he showed you pictures of your half-sisters?' Amy asked.

'And half-brother,' Gina reminded her. 'That was the weirdest thing. The really weird thing. There are these three people, my two twin sisters, a brother Menzie's age and no one even thought to tell me! No one thought I might be interested, or would like to see them or anything! I mean, it's just so incredibly selfish of everyone, but especially my mom. At least my real dad feels a bit guilty, a bit sorry.'

'I'm sure your mom does too. Didn't she apologize to you about six times when we were down there at the poolside talking about it?'

'Yeah, well she might be a bit sorry now, but all this time has gone by and she never once thought about how I might like to get to know Pieter and those other kids. My whole other family! I think he tried to get in touch before. He just wasn't sure whether to call my mom, or contact me directly.'

Suddenly Gina remembered something else he'd told her: 'He sent the candy. Do you remember the parcel of US candy? At the boarding house?'

Amy nodded.

'He sent it. He was going to sign his name, but then he suddenly thought that might be too weird, so he just sent the candy anyway. He had been eating Reese's Pieces and he'd thought of me. Isn't that bizarre? Apparently, none of his other kids like them.'

'Wow. So he'd been thinking of you, just like you'd been thinking of him.'

'I guess.'

'I wonder if my mum ever thinks about me.'

'Of course she does. How could she not?'

'I wonder if she has other children. I could have brothers and sisters too . . .' Amazingly, this thought had only just occurred to Amy. Fifteen years of her life she'd thought of herself as an only child, but there could be brothers and sisters just absolutely dying to meet her. Just like for Gina.

'Yes!' Gina said, excited for her. 'There could be another family for you too.'

'But it's how to break the ice, how to get started. I mean, I'm not exactly going to be able to hang out in restaurants in Glasgow and hope that I bump into her the way you bumped into your dad.'

'No. I guess not. I mean, I still can't believe I met him like that. But he was planning to call Mom anyway.'

'How am I going to find her?'

'You'll have to ask your dad, or maybe even your grandmother.'

'Oh, Gran would only tell me if she'd OK'd it with my dad first.'

'Well, maybe you'll just have to ask your dad.'

'This is a big thing . . . I really don't know how he's going to react to it.'

Niffy's voice called to them from the other side of the bedroom door: 'Last chance for a trip to the beach! Last chance before Scotland!'

Gina turned to Amy and told her, 'When you get back to Glasgow, ask him. If you don't ask, you'll never know.'

Chapter Twenty-seven

Amy breathed in the cold, clear air and fastened the strap under her helmet. This was fantastic, this was the life. She tucked her snowboard under her arm and followed her dad to the ski lift.

'So the family finances are improving a little, are they?' she asked as her dad leaned against the lift and began to travel up the snow-covered hill.

'Well, we're skiing in a shed, not in the Alps,' he replied with a wink.

'I had noticed.'

'But no, it's not looking too gloomy. Try not to worry about it, OK? I'm sure things are going to get much better.'

This may have been a shed, south of Glasgow, but it was a shed filled with real snow, and the slope was big and just scary and tricky enough to get down to provide a real thrill. Amy loved it when her dad brought her here.

At the start of the year, things had gone very badly for her dad's business. He'd once owned a string of nightclubs in Glasgow and several other big cities. But because of money problems, he'd had to sell up everything except the one club which was now keeping her in school, her dad in a rented flat, and paying for the odd treat like a snowboarding session.

Not to mention pocket money for California and the dinner at Wonky's – though when Amy had signed for the bill, she'd realized straight away that had been for much less than the menu prices: mates' rates, indeed.

The ski lift brought them right to the very top of the hill, where for a few moments they had to queue behind the other boarders and skiers waiting for their turn to take off.

Then Amy and her dad took their places. The slope was wide enough for them both to go down together. She set her board down and slipped her boots under the straps.

'On the count of three,' her dad said, shooting her a grin.

'One . . .' Amy began, grinning back. She wondered how many other St Jude's girls would be going snowboarding with their dads this holiday. This was definitely one of the big advantages of having such a young dad. He was a daredevil who liked to do exciting things, and he made life lots of fun for her.

'Two . . .' her dad said.

'Three!' Amy finished and launched herself down the slope.

Oh! Oh! Oh! The first time was always the worst. After a few goes, you got used to the speed, the balancing, the *whizzzzzzz*, the freezing air streaming past your cheeks.

Whoa! She wobbled. But stayed upright.

Her dad was speeding ahead of her now, bending his knees side to side, riding the curves.

Amy jumped the little mound of snow ahead of her, swerved slightly left, then right, then – wobble, tip, *whhhaaaaaah*, crunch – she fell straight into the soft heaps of snow at the bottom of the hill.

'Wipeout!' her dad teased. He stood over her and offered a hand to pull her up.

'Owwww!' Amy moaned, but once she was on her feet, nothing hurt as badly as she thought it might.

'Bruised your pride, have you?' her dad asked.

'Totally!' But she picked up her board and told him, 'Last one to the ski lift's a big girl's blouse.'

On their second run, Amy was delighted to see her

dad take a tumble two-thirds of the way down and roll for most of the rest of the way.

The third attempt, they both managed perfectly. Same with the fourth, but on the fifth run, Amy fell off down near the bottom again, and this time gave her ankle a vicious twist.

'Owwww!' She stood up and hobbled a little. 'I don't think I can go back up.'

'You can move your foot and everything OK?' her dad asked, looking worried.

'Yes. Ouch! It just hurts. I think it's a twist or a sprain, though. It's not major.'

'Hot chocolate time then,' he said, and put his arm under hers and around her back to help her hop to the changing rooms.

When they were out of their ski suits and sitting in a cosy booth with mugs of creamy chocolate in front of them, Amy began the conversation she'd been working up to ever since she'd returned from California.

'Gina's dad, her real dad, suddenly turned up in her life when we were there. In fact, it was in Wonky's restaurant.'

'Really? He's a great guy, the Wonk; I could tell you all sorts of mad and crazy things about him.'

But Amy wasn't going to be sidetracked. 'Gina went

for lunch with her real dad, who she hadn't seen since she was small, and they got on great and now she's going to go and spend some time with him in the summer . . . and meet her sisters and brother she didn't even know about!'

Her dad picked up his mug and took a long, thoughtful sip. 'It's delicious stuff,' he said, meaning the hot chocolate.

'Dad! Can you stop trying to change the subject?'

Her dad turned to look at her and gave a long sigh. 'I know where this is going and I don't like it. That's the problem,' he said.

'I've never wanted to find out about Mum before, but now . . . I think I'd like to know more than I do.'

Another sigh. Another long sip of chocolate.

'I know that you pay her a monthly allowance,' Amy blurted out.

Gary McCorquodale looked at his daughter in astonishment. 'How do you know about that?' he asked.

'When we were moving out of the flat . . . I saw some bank statements and I recognized the name.' Amy hung her head and felt guilty.

'You shouldn't have . . .' her dad began.

'No. I know, I know. I didn't mean to, I wasn't

looking. I just saw and I've been meaning to ask you. But I just haven't found the right moment. It's never the right moment.'

'No.' Her dad turned back to his cup and took another sip, and even though Amy was desperate to say something to encourage him to talk, she knew that she shouldn't. She needed to be quiet and wait now.

There was a long silence.

Finally her dad began with, 'Your mum has a lot of problems.'

Amy held her breath and waited for more.

'I send her a bit of money because I think I should, but I don't send her much because she would just use it in the wrong way.'

'What do you mean?'

'She's a heavy drinker . . . and I think there are drugs too.'

Amy chewed on her lip. She knew her mum and dad had been teenagers when she'd been born and that her mum hadn't stuck around to look after her for long. In fact, she couldn't remember ever having met her mum. She had really been brought up by her dad and her gran. She'd gone to boarding school at eleven, because her dad was out at work most nights and Amy had found being at home with her gran all the time a bit boring.

But in all the daydreams she'd had about her mum, she'd never for a moment considered that she might be an alcoholic . . . or worse.

She knew her dad and her gran didn't like her mum and always tried to avoid talking about her. But she'd thought this was because they didn't like the fact that she'd abandoned Amy. She'd never thought it was because her mum was some great big problem.

'When did you last see her?' Amy asked.

'About ten years ago.'

'Did she have those problems then?'

'Yeah. Really bad. I paid for her to go into rehab. In fact, I've paid for that three times now.'

'Did she get better?'

'For a short time, but she always seems to fall back into it.'

'Do you hear about her? Do you know where she lives? Or how she's doing?'

'Not really.'

'So you just send money . . . Are you sure she gets it?'

'Well, it goes into her bank account. As far as I know, she gets it.'

'Do you know how I could get in touch with her?'

Another sigh. Finally her dad said, 'What I don't

know is why you'd want to. I don't think anything good can come of it.'

'She's my mother!' Amy exclaimed, now feeling totally exasperated. 'Surely I'm allowed to meet my own mother?' Heads were turning in their direction, and Amy dropped her voice immediately. She didn't want to cause any kind of scene. 'At least tell me that you'll think about it,' she hissed at her dad.

'OK. OK.' He paused.

Amy felt her fingers clench. Was he going to let her find her mum?

'I'll think about. I promise to think about it.'

Chapter Twenty-eight

On the day before the summer term began at St Jude's, girls were arriving back to the boarding house from holidays all over the country and, in fact, from all over the globe.

Taxis from the airport ferried pupils exhausted by long-haul flights. Other girls met up on trains and shared the fare from the station. Large cars were also purring in through the gates, dropping off the girls who lived within driving distance of the school.

But Niffy made her way to the boarding house by foot, wheeling a medium-sized suitcase behind her. The Nairn-Bassett finances were completely precarious at best, so she'd told her parents to leave their clapped-out car in the garage and let her travel from Cumbria to Edinburgh by bus.

Not far from Edinburgh bus station, she'd heaved her bag onto a bus out towards the boarding house, and she was now making the last part of the trip by foot, limping a bit because her redwood injury was still healing.

She recognized most of the girls unloading stuff from car boots in the driveway and said a cheery hello as she passed. She hauled the bag up the stone steps at the front of the Victorian building and pushed open the heavy glass and wood front door.

'Hello, Luella, welcome back.' Mrs Knebworth was stationed in the hallway, as always at the start of a new term, meeting and greeting all the girls and their parents. 'Did you have a lovely holiday? You were in California with Gina and the others, weren't you?'

'Yes, thanks. Totally fantastic. It was an adventure. And so sunny. Every day! Once I got back, the rest of the holiday was generally pants and so gloomy I thought I should be going around with a torch.'

'I'm sure.' Mrs Knebworth smiled, but Niffy had known her long enough to see that there was something not quite right about that smile. It was just a little tight at the edges. The Neb's eyes weren't smiling either; they looked cold and beady.

They were boring right into Niffy, and Niffy just knew – right there and then – what this was all about.

A new girl and her parents were opening the front door now, so Mrs Knebworth had to turn her attention to them, but before she let Niffy go, she shot her an ominous: 'Can we have a little chat, Luella? Please come to my room at seven p.m.'

'No problem,' Niffy assured her, and hurried off down the corridor.

Up in the Iris dorm, she found Min already completely unpacked and about to go off to the study to do some homework.

'But we can't have any homework yet, we've not been to school,' Niffy protested.

'Well, you know what I mean. I've got a really great new biology book from my mum and I can't wait to get started. How's your foot, by the way?'

Niffy kicked away her shoe, peeled off her sock and showed it to Min proudly. 'Almost completely healed in just two weeks. Not bad, huh? I think I have you to thank for that.'

Min laughed. 'Not exactly. I think the medical team at the most expensive private hospital in Malibu may have played a little part.'

'No. It was all you. If that stick had stayed in any longer, who knows what might have happened. You were really brave.'

'I was brave?! Niff, when I think about it, I can still hear your scream.'

'There are probably birds that still haven't dared go back into those trees.'

'Not to mention hikers.'

'Min, you didn't pass out. Did it occur to you that maybe you've got over the fainting thing, and maybe you could be a doctor?'

'Ha! My little brother had a nosebleed last week and I was out cold on the kitchen floor. So I don't know how I managed with you that day. I think because you were so brave, you helped me to be brave too.'

'Sweet. How are your bugs?'

'The one in the restaurant died. I think Lorelei might have put too much pressure on his thorax.'

'That can probably happen when you're trying to get a cockroach out of the swankiest restaurant in town and you just happen to spot your ex-husband sitting at the next table.'

'But it was sort of a good thing, because I could bring him home, whereas I let the other two go.'

'You brought the roach home?' Niffy asked, popping open the locks on her case. A huge tumble of barely folded clothes spilled out onto the bed.

Min raised her eyebrows – everything in her drawers was washed, ironed and immaculately folded – but she didn't say anything, just moved over to Niffy's bed and began to help with the folding.

'Yes, I took the roach home. I studied him more closely under the microscope and I researched and I posted and I Googled, but I can't find another roach anywhere quite like him.'

'Weird.'

'He's blue. He's definitely a blue and brown roach.'

'Lovely . . .' Niffy tried to sound enthusiastic.

'I think he and his friends could be unique.'

'Really?'

'Yeah. I've written to the US Entomological Society to see if they can give me any more information.'

'Cool.' Niffy flicked a glance at her watch: five to seven. 'Where are Gina and Aim, by the way?'

'Gina's at Heathrow, her flight up has been delayed. Aim's having a pizza with her dad and not arriving back till eight, apparently.'

'And how do you know all this?'

'I have a new mobile.' Min took the gadget out of her pocket and wiggled it in front of Niffy's face.

'Me too,' Niffy said, and waved a phone card loaded

up with £10 in front of Min's face. 'And now, I have to go and see the Neb.'

'Oh no. Is it about . . . ?'

'Could be.'

'*Oh no!*'

Just one minute after seven, Niffy tapped on the door of Mrs Knebworth's sitting room.

'Is that Luella?'

'Yes.'

'Come in.'

Niffy pushed open the door, then shut it firmly behind her. If they were going to talk about what she thought they were going to talk about, then Niffy didn't want anyone else eavesdropping.

'Please take a seat,' Mrs Knebworth instructed, sitting down heavily in her own armchair. 'You left something on your bed at the end of last term . . .' the housemistress began. She sounded tired. Behind her thick glasses and dusting of face powder, she also looked tired.

Niffy nodded.

'I was doing a last check of the dorms, making sure no one had left passports or purses or anything important behind, and I found a local newspaper cutting on your bed . . .'

'My mum sent it because my horse was in the paper.'

Mrs Knebworth managed a little smile and nod at this. 'But there was another story on the back,' the housemistress went on.

Now it was Niffy's turn to nod.

'Did you realize who that story was about?'

'I wasn't totally sure,' Niffy admitted quietly, 'but I thought it might be.'

'Don't you think you should have brought that story to my attention?'

Niffy took a glance around the room. It was so neat and tidy: not one speck of dust, the photos on the mantelpiece all in a completely straight row. She'd been told off in this room so often in the past that it didn't exactly hold good memories for her.

'I wasn't sure it was the same man. Plus . . . I didn't think you'd believe me,' she said.

'Well, Luella, maybe if you'd not played so many jokes on me in the past . . .' Mrs Knebworth left it there.

'Hmmmmm,' Niffy murmured. Saying sorry would be a step too far. Some of those jokes had been really good, and well-deserved.

'So you left the newspaper where you thought I might find it; was that the plan?'

Niffy gave a slight shrug then she admitted, 'I didn't want to bring it to you. But I didn't want to just throw it away without telling you, so . . . yes . . . I hoped you'd find it and decide what to do.'

'Who else knew about the newspaper?'

'Just the dorm and I know – they haven't told anyone else. We all understood how serious it could be.'

Mrs Knebworth drew her mouth into a tight line and Niffy was sure that a blistering lecture was about to spill out and she would be doing chores in the boarding house for the rest of her time at St Jude's.

But instead, Mrs Knebworth sighed, then she looked down at her skirt and picked an imaginary piece of fluff from it.

'Well, Luella, I almost hate to say this, but it seems that for once, you may actually have done the right thing. I appreciated being on my own, away from any prying eyes when I found out about this. As you can imagine, it's been a difficult holiday for me . . .' She was picking at the imaginary fluff again.

'Was it the same man?' Niffy asked quietly.

'Oh yes. He's been sentenced now. Two months in

prison and he'll have to repay the people he cheated.'
Mrs Knebworth kept her face turned down towards her
skirt as she said this.

'Oh . . . my . . . goodness,' Niffy managed.

'Yes. Well, obviously I feel like I've been cheated too.
He didn't take my money, but I still feel robbed.'

Niffy realized she actually felt sorry for Mrs
Knebworth, and it was such a strange and unusual
feeling that she had no idea what to say. She was pretty
sure Mrs Knebworth would not want anyone at all
feeling sorry for her.

'That's terrible.'

'Yes. But there we are. The main thing is that no
one found out that there was a connection between
that man and the St Jude's housemistress. You
know how very important the reputation of the
school is to me. It is the most important thing in the
world. I've been a part of this school for almost my
entire life now. I would never do anything that might
harm it.'

'No. Everyone knows that.'

'Thank you, Luella. As I say, for once you do appear
to have done the right thing. Now, I know there will be
lots of gossip about where Mrs Knebworth's gentleman
caller has gone. I would appreciate it if you and your

friends could keep the information contained in the newspaper entirely to yourselves.'

There was no mistaking the steel in the blue eyes now. This was a command which Niffy and her friends would have to obey. Or else the Neb would make the consequences too terrible to even think about.

Chapter Twenty-nine

'Have you heard about Penny B-H?' Amy asked Gina, just as soon as she caught up with her outside their maths class.

'No. What's she done now?'

'She's organizing the Upper Fifth summer dance. The whole thing! She and her friends are making it a charity fundraising event, instead of just a social. She's been to the Banshee, had it all approved and now she could win the best fundraising idea prize!'

Gina wasn't particularly concerned about this. She had lots of other things to think about – including her new boyfriend who she was supposed to see tomorrow. But she could see that Amy was really upset about it.

'Does it really matter?' she asked. 'So what if she wins the best fundraising prize? Is it really such a big deal?'

Amy's face turned sulky. 'Yes! We were going to come

up with a great idea. We were at least going to give her a run for her money.'

Gina shrugged. 'Maybe we're too busy.'

'Maybe we've not got any good ideas. Plus, she's hijacked the dance. The whole thing will be Penny-ish. A complete Boswell-Hackett fest. And apparently she's raising funds for some trust that preserves ancient buildings! I mean, come on, that's not orphans, is it? We were supposed to raise money for orphans.'

'Amy,' Gina hissed, as their teacher had now opened the door and was ushering them into the class, 'you've not mentioned this once. Not once during the whole holidays. Is it really about raising money? Or is it all about getting back at Penny?'

Amy didn't reply; she just stomped into the room and deliberately sat as far away from Gina as she could. Gina found herself sitting beside Posy, one of the day girls she really liked.

'Have you and Amy fallen out?' Posy wondered.

'No. Amy's upset because she just found out that Penny is running the summer dance to raise funds.'

'But that's a good idea,' Posy said, pushing her dark hair behind her ears and opening her textbook at the page Mrs Cable, the maths teacher, had instructed.

'I know,' Gina whispered, 'but Amy is always totally

jealous when Penny gets something that she hasn't got, or does something that she hasn't done, or gets any kind of success at all. It's a really intense rivalry and I'm not sure any of the rest of us will ever really get it.'

Posy rolled her eyes, and just before they dived into the first algebra question of the day, she told Gina, 'Amy won't be too pleased about Penny's new boyfriend then.'

'Huh? She has a new boyfriend?'

'Yeah, they started going out in the Easter holidays, some guy from Saint Lennox. Jason something?'

'Not Jason Hernandez?'

Posy frowned and repeated the name. 'I think that's it. Apparently he's tall, dark-haired and really, really good-looking.'

'OMG,' Gina scribbled down on the corner of her maths book, because Mrs Cable's glare was on them now. 'Jason Hernandez is Amy's ex. She will go *nuclear*!!'

Chapter Thirty

By 7.08 p.m. on Saturday evening, Gina decided that despite her high-heeled ankle boots and her carefully done hair, she would have to start running up the Lothian Road to get to her date on time.

Yes, even if running meant she would sweat and sweating would spoil her beautifully applied make-up. She was late. She was fourteen minutes late so far, and she didn't know if Callum would wait for her that long.

Callum!!!

She couldn't wait to see him. Suddenly it wasn't hard to run in two-inch heels because she really, really wanted to be with him.

ON WAY XX

LATE!! XX

She'd texted him twice, but there had been no reply yet. The thought that he might not be there waiting for her much longer made her steps even quicker.

Where was he?!

Why wasn't he replying on his phone?

Now she could see the Filmhouse Theatre and she began to scan the faces of the people waiting outside. He wasn't there . . . Where was he? Her heart began to jump with anxiety in her chest.

Maybe inside . . .

Carefully, in the heels, she took the flight of steps up to the door and walked into the brightly lit lobby.

'Gina!'

And there he was!

'Gina, you made it.'

'Sorry, I texted but—'

She was scooped up, pressed in against his leather jacket and kissed right on the mouth in a way that made her forget in a moment that she was right in the middle of a crowded cinema lobby.

'Sorry, my phone's died,' he said, and kissed her again. 'You are looking fantastic. Great dress.' He actually stepped back and admired her from top to toe, then swooped in and kissed her hungrily again.

Now she felt blushing and breathless.

'Let's forget about the film. It looks queued out

anyway.' He put his arm around her waist and pulled her in close.

'What shall we do instead?' Gina asked, although this was breaking a second school rule.

Number one rule was that you could only go out with boys the housemistress had actually met and approved. She'd told Mrs Knebworth she was going to the cinema with Dermot, as friends.

Number two rule was you had to be where you said you were going to be.

Breaking the rules and getting caught by Mrs Knebworth could land you in a whole world of trouble.

'Let's just get out of here and walk . . . until we see somewhere that we'd like to be. I want to hear all about your holiday. I want to taste a lot more lip gloss, baby.' He slid his hands down from Gina's waist onto her behind as he said this, and she couldn't help giving a little squeak of excitement.

'Where are we?'

'OK, just put your foot here, jump up, swing over and I'll be right behind you.'

Gina scrambled over the iron railing and landed in her high heels on the soft, damp grass below. She and

Callum had walked, talked, held hands and kissed all the way from the Filmhouse to here.

But where was here?

They were in a quiet, old, old street – the kind of Edinburgh street that made Gina think she was on a film set or had somehow been taken back in time. There were old-fashioned street lanterns burning a dim orange in the darkness, and the place they'd just snuck into, over the iron railings, was even darker, with no street lights at all.

'Is this a garden?' Gina asked, her heels sinking into the grass as they moved forward.

'No,' Callum said. His voice sounded full of fun. 'This is a graveyard . . . *mwahhh ha, ha, ha, haaaaa!*' He gave his best horror laugh but Gina just smacked his arm.

'You're kidding right?'

'No. Have a look. This isn't a little stone building, it's a tomb.'

Gina looked up at an elaborate carved urn on the top. It wasn't like any kind of gravestone she'd seen before, but now she totally believed him. 'Why have you brought me to a graveyard?' she asked, feeling a little bit creeped out about it.

'Because it's private, it's quiet. No one will bother us.'

He turned to her, put his arms around her waist and moved in for a kiss.

'But what do you mean?' she asked, pulling back from him. 'It's creepy here and it's cold.'

'Just snuggle up, baby. I promise to keep you very, very warm.' He pulled her in tighter.

Gina began to kiss him, but it didn't feel right. It didn't feel hot or exciting or adventurous. It felt a little scary. He was holding her too tightly. He was kissing too hard. They were in this creepy place, so far away from anyone else. She felt frightened. But she kept telling herself that she was just being silly, she was imagining things. This was Callum. He was fine. He was fun.

Callum's hand moved down onto her behind. He pulled her in towards him, then his hand moved down her leg and . . . Was his hand moving in under her dress?

She put her hand on his, stopping any further movement. Maybe if they were on a warm sofa in a friendly familiar house, she would be fine with this. She would be curious to know what was going to happen next.

But she was in a graveyard . . . at night . . . and she didn't know her way back from here.

It was creepy.

'That's enough,' she said.

'C'mon,' Callum urged. 'Let's have some fun.' He burrowed his face against her neck and began to kiss her there. His hand was still trying to move further up her leg.

'No, this is not fun.' Gina pulled away. 'I didn't ask you to take me to some creepy graveyard. I'm cold. I'm breaking two school rules at least, and I want to go back.'

'C'mon,' Callum tried once again.

Now Gina felt properly annoyed, not scared or creeped out. 'Take me back!' she stormed, and stamped on his foot.

'OWWW!'

This made Callum let go of her. Gina turned and marched towards the railings. She didn't run because she wasn't frightened of him; she was just annoyed.

Why had he brought her here?

'Who wants to make out in a cemetery?' she asked. 'It's creepy and weird.' She put her foot up on the railing and lifted herself back over, snagging the back of her dress and hearing a slight rip as she went.

Oh, just great.

'You better be following, because you're going to take

me to the nearest road where I can get a cab,' she said, her bossy confidence coming directly from how annoyed she was.

Callum was just messing with her. She suspected he wanted more from her than she had even thought about giving. Plus, he didn't even seem that interested in her tonight. Now that she thought about it, all the way over here, he'd asked her just two questions, then talked entirely about himself.

And, of course, he'd had to tell her all about Dermot's new girlfriend.

'He's going out with Caitlyn from his English class. She has short hair and a wonky nose,' he'd said. 'She has been after him for months. Poor man, I don't think he stood a chance. She's got some friend at Saint Jude's who knew you were dumping him, and she started texting him the same day.'

'Oh. Well . . . I'm sure she's just fine,' Gina had said, feeling she had to stick up for poor Dermot.

Callum shook his head. 'No, nooooo, no. Into very heavy poetry and Leonard Cohen.'

'And how do you know?'

'I've escaped her clutches.'

At the time Gina had laughed, but now that she remembered the comment, it seemed such a show-off thing to say. Of course Caitlyn had wanted Callum first, because Callum was just so great, wasn't he?

He climbed over the railing now and stood where he landed, hands in pockets looking sulky.

'The nearest road where I can hail a cab, please,' she said frostily.

He shrugged and began to walk. She walked beside him, but there was a gap of about a metre between them now. And silence.

A deep silence. Gina waited, wondering what Callum might say. She didn't want to be the first to talk. She'd said enough.

Maybe he'd like to apologize or something?

Maybe he was just going to let them walk on in this sulky huff?

Four or five long minutes went by. Now she could hear traffic in the distance, and they were moving out of the quiet, winding side streets towards a main road.

Finally she couldn't stand the silence any more. 'Don't you want to say something?' she asked.

'Like what?' came the immediate reply.

'Like maybe: *Sorry for taking you to some lonely, spooky graveyard.*'

Callum shrugged. 'Other girls haven't minded.

They've thought it was fun.'

'Fun! Fun? Your idea of fun is warped. Undressing in a cinema? Feeling me up in a graveyard.'

Callum shrugged again. 'Other girls—'

'Shut up! Not helping!' Gina exclaimed.

'Here's the road. In fact, there's a taxi,' Callum said, sticking his hand up in the air.

Gina gave a gasp of exasperation. 'Is that it? You're gonna hail me a cab and we're not going to say anything else about tonight?'

'Yeah.'

The taxi was pulling over.

'Fine,' Gina stormed. 'Goodnight!' With that, she got into the taxi, slammed the door shut and didn't turn to look at Callum again.

She was so totally over him.

'Where are we off to?' the taxi driver asked.

'Ummmmm . . .' Gina hesitated. It was too early to go back to the boarding house. She'd have to explain why she hadn't stayed till the end of the film. Too complicated.

'The Filmhouse please,' she decided.

'Not exactly far away, is it?' the taxi driver complained.

Within a few minutes they were there and Gina paid

the small fare. The queue had disappeared; obviously all the films had started now and it would be too late to get a ticket, but she could go to the bar, drink a coffee, calm down and head back to the boarding house in forty minutes or so.

She walked through the cinema lobby, unprepared for how packed it was, even though the films were playing. Every single table was taken; people were leaning against the walls, the bar was crammed with queuing drinkers. It was going to take several minutes to order a coffee and find a spare table.

As she queued up at the bar to make her order, she glanced over the packed tables, searching for a spare seat, and all of a sudden she was looking straight at Dermot and he was looking right back.

He smiled, raised his hand and mouthed, 'Hi.'

'Hi,' she replied. For a moment she just stood there, wondering if she should go and say hello or just stay here in the queue. But then Dermot gestured for her to come over.

As she got towards the table, he smiled and asked, 'Have you found him yet?'

'Ummm . . .'

Gina could feel her heart speed up. It was too weird to see Dermot sitting here, in a T-shirt and jacket, looking cool, looking handsome . . . a cup of coffee in front of him and . . .

Gina had a moment now to take in the scene properly. A really cute girl with short dark hair, smoky eyes and yes, maybe a charmingly wonky nose, was sitting right beside him – way too close to be just a friend.

Dermot was on a *date*!

Well, why not? She was seeing someone else . . . it had been weeks since they broke up . . . this had to be Caitlyn. But it still felt strange to see him here with someone else.

Gina had to blink hard, because she could feel the very beginning of tears start up behind her eyes. Dermot had been such a good friend, and now she wondered if she would ever be able to go back to his café and have a laugh with him. Or were they supposed to pretend to be strangers from now on?

'Are you looking for Callum?' Dermot asked.

'No . . . no. I've seen him and . . . well . . . it didn't really go great. I think the Callum thing is finished.'

'Oh . . . sorry. He is a bit of a prat,' was Dermot's verdict.

Gina shrugged and smiled. 'I think you might be right,' she replied. She couldn't read anything from Dermot's voice. It sounded completely calm, as if bumping into her like this was totally fine for him.

'Sorry, I'm being rude. This is Caitlyn. Caitlyn, meet Gina. I'm not giving anyone labels here, because that might be really awkward.'

Caitlyn smiled at Gina, and Gina gave a little laugh. Dermot was cracking jokes. It was OK. Maybe they could just move straight into being friends without any big drama. Caitlyn held out her hand and for a moment or two Gina found herself shaking hands with Dermot's new girlfriend.

'Did you want a coffee?' Dermot offered.

'No, I've changed my mind,' Gina said immediately, because sitting here with the two of them just wouldn't be right. They were on a date. They didn't need her around. She gave an exaggerated look at her watch. 'I should head back.' She couldn't help herself from looking right into his eyes, hoping to find a little trace that he was sorry, hoping he could read that she was a little sorry too.

But . . . they were both going to have to be big. People broke up all the time. They moved on.

'Nice to see you,' Gina said, making her smile as charming as she could and flashing it at Caitlyn too.

'Yeah . . .' Dermot managed to raise a little grin at this too. 'Come in and have a coffee some time. You know where to find me.'

Gina's smile broadened at the peace offering.

'I will, thanks. Have a good night.'

Chapter Thirty-one

When Min and Gina walked into the boarding house together on Monday after school, they looked on the little mail table behind the front door and were both astonished to see there was something for each of them.

A large brown padded envelope had *Miss Gina Peterson* typed out on the front.

A long white envelope of thick, expensive-looking paper with US stamps was addressed to Miss Asimina Singupta.

'Cool!' Gina said, picking up the parcel. 'I love getting mail!'

'Oh my!' Min exclaimed, reading the postmark on her letter. 'I think they've written back.'

They both headed for the dining room where freshly baked cakes were always set out as a back-from-school treat. Once they'd each put two fairy cakes on their plates and poured out tea, they sat down at a table to examine their mail.

Gina ripped open her parcel and was delighted to find a bubble-wrapped selection of the best kind of American candy inside. 'Reese's Pieces ... Hershey's Kisses ... grape-flavoured gum! This is amazing. Even more stuff than the first time ...' She delved in further and pulled out a piece of typed paper. It was from the company which had sent out the treats. It listed the order in detail and there at the bottom was a typed-out message:

'*Gina, just in case you were missing candy from home. See you in the summer, love Pieter,*' she read out.

'Is that your other dad?' Min asked.

'Other dad?' Gina smiled. 'Good way of putting it. Yeah. Nice of him, huh? He sent the last package, but it was unsigned that time. It's all been mailed from Britain. He's obviously discovered some online company over here that can mail you US candy. Cool. What about you? You've not even got the envelope open yet. C'mon!'

Min's finger slid along the top of the envelope gingerly. 'It says on the back it's from the American Entomological society.'

'The bug people?'

'Yes ... I wrote to them about the blue cockroaches. I sort of presented my evidence and I wanted to know if they had any further information.'

'Oh, boy. Well, c'mon, let's see what they say.'

'I feel a bit nervous ...' Min still hadn't got the letter out of the envelope.

'C'mon,' Gina urged, 'or I'm going to get hold of that letter and read it myself.'

'OK, OK.' Min reached for the single page of paper inside and unfolded it. She didn't read it out loud; she scanned over it silently as Gina tried to read her expression.

'Well?' Gina asked impatiently.

'Shhh ... I have to read it again,' Min said in a hushed voice.

Gina gave her a minute or two and then asked again, '*Well?!* What does it say?'

Min moved the page away from her face and now Gina could see the astonished smile she was wearing.

'It says ... it says they have no record of any insect like mine. They would like me to send over further specimens and they are going to investigate further. Do you know what this *means*?'

'You've discovered a blue bug?'

'I've discovered some sort of genetically different variant ... it could be environment, it could be contamination, it could be soil, breeding conditions ... there are all sorts of factors which could have given rise to the possibly minute population of blue cockroach.'

'Right ...' Gina said, a little hesitantly. She wasn't sure if she'd understood much of that. 'So that's good, isn't it? You've found a new variant of bug.'

'Good? Yes! It's very, very exciting. I'm going to have to go and tell Greg! And my mum and dad and Zarah, who's been looking in the microscope too. This could go on my CV, Gina,' Min said, wide-eyed, standing up from her seat. 'This could help me get to Cambridge. I mean – a new cockroach variant ...' In a tiny whisper, she added, 'They might even name it after me!'

'Wow ... and to think that I got all excited back there about a bag of candy.'

Min shot off with her letter, leaving Gina to clear away their plates and mugs. Once she'd finished, Gina picked up her bag of candy and went in search of the girl she knew would totally appreciate it – Niffy.

* * *

Niffy was stretched out on her bed in the dorm, halfway through the book she'd chosen for her personal study: *The Old Man and the Sea*.

'How's it going?' Gina asked as she came into the room.

'Fine,' Niffy replied. 'I'm at sea. I'm trying to catch a very, very big fish.'

'*Moby Dick*?' Gina wondered.

'Ah . . . now that's a good point. Is *The Old Man and the Sea* Hemmingway's homage to *Moby Dick*? I hadn't thought about that. Mrs Parker is going to be mucho, mucho impressed.'

'Would you like some candy?'

Niffy closed the book, sat up, looked at Gina expectantly and said, 'Now you're talking. What have you got? My top two sweets of all time are Crunchies and toffees, but I am prepared to eat pretty much anything you've got, except for Parma Violets or anything with sherbet. I mean, a line has to be drawn.'

Gina laughed. 'I've got another bag of US candy,' she said, tipping it out over her bed. 'Take whatever you like the look of.'

'Blimey!' was Niffy's reaction to the pile of gleaming, brightly wrapped goodies. She came over and began to search through the treats, looking for things that appealed. 'Menzie sent this, didn't he? Because we were talking about US and UK sweets and I promised to send him over a selection of ours. I mean, he's never tried a Smartie. How can you get to ten and never have tried a Smartie?'

'It'll melt,' Gina warned her. 'US chocolate tastes different because it melts at a higher temperature.'

'I didn't realize there was such a science to it, but it's a good science. Maybe I could get into it.'

'My new dad sent these,' Gina said.

'Oh . . .' Niffy was unwrapping a Hershey's Kiss and was a little distracted.

'I thought you were going to be a show-jumper?' Gina reminded her.

'Three-day eventer,' Niffy corrected, biting down on the chocolate, 'but sweet inventor would be good too. Chocolate taster . . . Do you think you can be a professional chocolate taster?'

'Probably.'

'Mmmmm. This is good.'

'Have a Reece's. Chocolate and peanut butter. It's a really amazingly brilliant combination.'

'I bet. So these have been sent all the way from the States?'

Gina shook her head and picked up the letter

which had come with the candy. 'No, looks like he found some British company online which mails US candy out to you. This was posted in Britain. Here it is: *www.uscandy4u.co.uk.*'

'This is very, very good,' Niffy decided, chewing slowly on the latest thing to go into her mouth. 'So we can order more? In fact, why don't we order loads and set up a stall? In fact . . .'

Niffy and Gina looked at each other, the brilliant idea now occurring to them both at the same time.

'A charity candy stall!' Gina blurted out.

'Exclusive treats you can't buy anywhere else!' Niffy added.

'That is a great idea!' they said both at the same time.

The dorm door swung open and Amy came in, scowling.

'Amy!' Gina exclaimed. 'We've just had the best fundraising idea ever. It's brilliant.'

'Genius,' Niffy added.

'You're gonna love it.'

'This will definitely give Penny B-H a run for her money,' Niffy added.

'Don't mention her. Don't even mention that girl's name to me. Have you heard who her new boyfriend is? Have you heard?' Amy sat down heavily on the edge of her bed, her face even more scowly and angry than before.

Gina and Niffy exchanged a glance. Both of them had found out last week, and neither of them had had the nerve to tell Amy, because even though she and Jason Hernandez had broken up ages ago, it was obviously still a big deal that Jason had now decided to go out with Penny.

'He was such a bad boyfriend to me. Don't you remember?' Amy asked.

Gina and Niffy both nodded. It seemed too risky to say anything.

'He never phoned...weeks would go by...we always had a good time when we were together... Now he's decided to go out with her! Her!! Why her?! And I just bet she's only going out with him because of me.'

'Amy, please stop it,' Gina began. 'Jason was a louse. Don't you remember he was going out with that other girl? Don't you remember all that? You were so upset about it. Please. Just forget about him. If Penny wants to give him a whirl, good luck to her. Ex-boyfriends! I now have two of them in this city. Time to say goodbye, good luck, and move on.'

'Huh! What's your great idea then?' Amy asked sulkily.

'See this pile of gorgeous goodies on my bed – dive in, by the way. It's all US candy, but sent by a British company, online. Niffy and I thought we could get a big delivery and set up an exclusive candy stall at school.'

Amy didn't say anything.

Gina thought that maybe this was because she knew it was a good idea, but she was in such a bad mood, she didn't even want to say it.

'*Hmmmmmpf. . .*' Amy managed finally. 'Suppose so. But I'm only going to help if we can run it for five days and make tons more money than Penny and her dance.'

'We'll try,' Gina said cheerfully, 'and that will be taking revenge for a good cause.'

'Ha! A candy stall is not my revenge . . . I'm going to have to do something much, much worse to get revenge.'

Chapter Thirty-two

'So you're really totally over him. He's not invited and you don't even really mind?' Niffy asked, as she slowly pulled the zipper up on a very, very pink, short ball dress.

'Callum? Do you mean Callum?' Gina asked, adding the finishing dab to her carefully lined, lipsticked and glossed lips.

Niffy nodded.

'I am totally finished and over him, can hardly remember his name. No idea what I saw in him.'

'Does this mean that the only one of us with a boyfriend at the dance is Min? That is strange. I mean, *Min*.'

Min was admiring her cute yellow dress in the mirror and assessing how well it went with the pair of purple shoes which Amy had lent her. She smiled. 'It's not a mystery, you know. I picked a really nice guy and we have lots in common.'

'So he's coming tonight, is he?' Gina asked.

'Yes, of course. But don't worry, you'll have fun hunting for new boys. They're coming from all over: Saint Lennox, Craigiefield and all the other places they keep the "nice young men", as Mrs K would say.'

'Aim, you're still not dressed. We have to go over there in about fifteen minutes.'

Amy looked at Niffy in the mirror as she tonged her hair into a cascade of ringlets. 'That is a very, very pink dress,' Amy said.

'I know. I borrowed it from Mel.'

'Mel?! How could you borrow anything from Mel? You'll probably catch something.'

'She's all right. Don't you think it looks good?'

'Come here,' Amy instructed.

Niffy, in the bright pink, slightly too low, slightly too short number, obeyed. Once she was at Amy's side, Amy put down the tongs and turned her attention on her friend. She took off Niffy's white bobble clip-on earrings with a snap.

'Ouch!' Niffy said.

'So mumsy.' Amy handed them to her.

'Yeah, they are actually my mum's.'

Around Niffy's neck, Amy fastened one of her brightest, chunkiest Accessorize purchases. 'Bit better,' she declared. Then she took a big glittery hair comb and swept back one side of Niffy's short and oddly dyed bob. A slick of bright pink lip gloss, a *swish swish* of blusher on each cheek, and finally Amy was happy to let Niffy go.

'Much better,' she declared. 'Obviously I can't do anything about your shoes, because I am not a size nine, or whatever it is you take these days.'

Everyone looked down at the white pumps Niffy was wearing.

'I borrowed these from Bronwen in Upper Six. Turns out she's a nine as well.'

Amy looked as if she was about to say something, but then she seemed to think better of it.

'Thanks,' Niffy said, looking herself over in the mirror. 'Definitely better. But what are you wearing?'

'I didn't get anything new,' Amy said immediately, 'because, you know, the family finances are improving, but I'm not ready to go on a spendathon just yet.' She opened her wardrobe door and a white petticoat adorned with white feathers peeped out from the side.

'Oooooh, are you wearing the amazing feathery princess dress?' Gina wanted to know.

'No, I think it's too much. This isn't a ball, it's a dance.

Plus, Penny B-H has seen the princess dress before, so she's bound to make some remark. So no, I'm going with leggings, my blue suede high heels and that lovely sequinned blue tunic, you remember, that I wore to—'

Gina groaned. 'No one remind me of that party . . . the red wine and Dermot and Charlie Fotheringham-Whatsit having their punch-up.'

'Yeah,' Amy said, 'that's the one. I think only Min had a good time at that party.'

'You all spoiled it for me!' Min pointed out.

'OK, OK, let's not go on about it,' Niffy chipped in. 'I know Angus and my brother are definitely not coming tonight, but is Charlie?'

'Oh no! You have got to be kidding?' Gina protested. 'He's coming? Why does he bother? So we can all spend the evening thinking up ruder and ruder things to say to him? He always calls me the Yank!'

'He probably likes you really,' Niffy said.

'Euuuuuw, you have got to be kidding.'

'Maybe he won't be there,' Min pointed out. 'No point getting worked up until you actually see him.'

Amy sprayed her curls into place and passed the powder brush over her face one last time. Then she slipped into her leggings and pulled the sparkly blue tunic dress out from the wardrobe. Finally she tied on the strappy, high-heeled shoes.

'Not going to be doing a lot of dancing in those,' Niffy remarked.

'I'll be fine. Just a bit wobbly for the first twenty minutes or so.'

'And very sore for the last twenty minutes or so,' Min said.

'You look amazing,' Gina told her. 'We're all just jealous.'

'Hey, we all look great,' Amy said generously. 'Gina, you are rocking the LBD, Min come over here, I just need to tong a curl or two next to your face and you will be delicious.'

'Time to go!' came the shout from the hallway.

'Time to go . . .' Amy repeated. She exchanged a glance with Niffy. 'Time to set the Penny B-H sabotage plan into action.'

'What? What plan?' Gina asked. 'Please, don't go and get yourself into a load of trouble over her.'

'Amy will be fine,' Niffy said. 'She is using the skills of a master saboteur.'

'Huh? Does that mean you, Niffy? Yeah, all your plans go so well. Look how it ended in California.'

'It ended amazingly! We got dinner in the best place

in town, Menzie met Will Smith and you ran into your other dad. That was all because of the flour bomb. No other explanation.'

'Amy,' Gina pleaded, 'don't do anything crazy. Please! It's for charity.'

'Gina, the tickets have all been paid for already and I won't interrupt the raffle. Other than that: she's fair game.'

Chapter Thirty-three

As other boarders went into the Upper Fifth cloakroom in the main school building to hang up their coats and change their shoes after the walk over from the boarding house, Niffy unloaded a suspiciously heavy bag from her shoulder.

'When do we strike?' Amy asked her in a whisper.

'Just as soon as we can. Might be best if we go up to the kitchen and offer to help.'

'There's no chance of bumping into P B-H up there? I mean she's going to be very suspicious if I turn up to help at her charity dance.'

Niffy shook her head: 'No, she's compere for the night. No chance of her being caught dead in the kitchen. She's put all the volunteers she doesn't like on drink and snack duty. I think Louisa's in charge of them. The rest of the inner circle got to decorate the hall and set up the raffle.'

'What's the theme in the hall?'

'Georgian buildings in distress.'

Amy snorted with laughter.

'Hey, I'm coming round to the idea,' Niffy retorted. 'Maybe my mum and dad can get a donation for Blacklough.'

'Well, just give me the stuff then and I'll go and do this job myself.'

'No! You'll do everything wrong without me.'

Amy was very happy for Niffy to come with her. She was worried about bumping into P B-H and having to come up with a cover story. No one was better at a cover story than Niffy.

'Follow me,' Niffy instructed.

They walked down several long school corridors, but at the bottom of the wide staircase, where most of the Upper Fives turned left to go towards the assembly hall, Amy and Niffy turned right and hurried up the stairs towards the kitchens.

As they walked through the empty dining room to the kitchen, Amy dropped back, trying to hide herself behind Niffy, but Niffy just kept on striding confidently forward.

'Are you sure she's not here?' Amy hissed.

'Can't see her,' Niffy replied. 'C'mon, just act

naturally.' She pushed open the swing doors and walked into the room, where five or six girls were busy arranging snacks on trays and pouring cartons of juice into several glass punchbowls. 'Hi,' she said cheerily. 'I've brought over a few things from the boarding-house kitchen. Compliments of Mrs Knebworth.'

One of the girls turned round at this, and Amy and Niffy saw that it was Louisa, one of Penny's best friends. She gave them a suspicious look.

'*You've* come to help out at Penny's charity dance?' she asked scornfully, looking directly at Amy.

'We're just bringing some things over from the boarding house,' Niffy answered. 'Anyway, you need to get stuff down there, everyone's arriving, Penny's in a flap.'

This was a guess, but it seemed to work as everyone immediately grabbed at a tray and headed for the door.

'Shall I set these things out too?' Niffy said, holding up her bag.

'Yes, OK,' Louisa said, picking up two plates of crisps and following the other girls out of the room.

Then Niffy and Amy were alone.

'Simple!' Niffy said with a smile.

'Unbelievable!' was Amy's verdict.

'C'mon, quick, we'd better get a move on.'

Amy set out two plates and Niffy poured the box of dog biscuits out on them. Niffy was the one who had picked out the exact brand of dog treats in the shop, assuring Amy that her pets ate these biscuits and she could never get over how like human snacks they looked.

'Oh my goodness,' Amy exclaimed as the biscuits were poured out. 'They really do look like proper biscuits.'

'But they do not taste like proper biscuits, believe me.'

'You haven't?!'

'Only a corner . . . only a crumb. Absolutely revolting.'

'Good,' Amy said, smoothing the assortment down over the plates.

'Next,' Niffy said, pulling a jar of chilli powder from her bag, followed by a jar of garlic salt.

They set to work sprinkling chilli and garlic over the remaining snacks. Niffy even dumped a good dose of chilli into the punch and stirred it in.

'And finally . . .' Niffy said, taking out the half bottle of vodka she'd bought at a monumental mark-up from her new fairy godmother, Mel.

'You did not!' Amy exclaimed. 'How did you get that?'

'Mel.'

'Brilliant.'

'But it's only a half bottle. Let's just dump it all into that small bowl there, so at least it will have a proper effect. No point pouring a little bit into every bowl.'

'OK, hurry, hurry!' Amy was sure she could hear footsteps coming up the stairs.

Niffy started pouring.

Now both of them could hear footsteps.

'Hurry!' Amy urged. She was already looking for a hiding place, just in case this was Penny. 'Over here!' she told Niffy.

Niffy poured out the last of the bottle, then dashed after Amy. They rounded a corner and squeezed themselves into a little alcove filled with mops, buckets and brooms.

'Come on, you take that tray. Louisa, if you take one of the punchbowls, I'll take this other one. Milly, can you manage that one? OK, then, just one more trip back up and we'll be done.'

It was Penny's voice.

Amy slid herself further back into the shadows at the sound of it. She did not want to be caught back here.

Penny would suspect immediately that something was up.

Slap! The unmistakable sound of liquid splashing down on the floor.

'Oh, Louisa!' Penny said angrily. 'Look what you've done! I'll need to get a mop.'

Now they could hear Penny's footsteps walking the length of the kitchen . . . turning the corner . . .

Niffy jumped out of the alcove, mop in hand. 'Were you looking for one of these?' she asked.

'What are *you* doing here?' Penny snapped.

'I brought some snacks over from the boarding house, then I poured myself a glass of water, spilled some . . .'

Penny snatched the mop from Niffy's hand. 'All right, we can manage without you. I think you'd better go downstairs.'

'Right . . .' Niffy said, sounding uncertain. 'Are you sure? I could do the mopping, you could take the punch and stuff down.'

'No. We'll be fine without your help,' Penny insisted.

'Right . . .'

All of a sudden there was a clanking, rattling, rolling noise from the direction of the mop store.

'What the hell was that?' Penny demanded, totally

tense and edgy with the stress of being the main hostess for the evening.

'Oh, I must have unbalanced something when I got the mop and it's fallen over. Don't worry, I'll sort it.' With that, Niffy darted back round the corner, just in time to see Amy dive behind one of the huge school cookers. Niffy picked up the metal bucket Amy had knocked over and put it back into the mop store, just as Penny walked round to see what she was doing. 'All set to rights,' she said cheerfully.

'Just go away now, will you?' Penny said. 'We can do without you.'

There was nothing for it. Niffy had to leave the kitchen, hoping that Penny and her friends wouldn't need to look behind the cooker for any reason.

Chapter Thirty-four

Crouched down behind the cooker, Amy listened hard.
When she was absolutely sure she couldn't hear anyone,
she got up and peeped into the area where the party
food had been laid out.

No one was there.

She quickly hurried to the door, went out into the
dining room and ran quickly down the stairs before
anyone could spot she'd been anywhere near Penny's
party goodies.

As she approached the assembly hall, she could hear
that the dance had already started up. There was the
loud hum of voices, plus the cheesy jazz band that
Penny had organized for the night had already begun
to play. Great big photographs of beautiful buildings
were being projected onto the walls, and a disco ball
was spinning high up on the ceiling, showering
the room with swirling lights. If Amy hadn't hated

Penny so much, she'd have had to admit that it looked great.

Against one of the walls, two long tables had been set out with food, punchbowls, plates and glasses. Amy could see Min giggling with Greg as he poured out a glass of punch for her. Just a glance at the punchbowl told Amy that it wasn't the one which had been doctored.

Greg handed Min the drink, then his fingers wandered to the dish nearest him and he picked up a big dog biscuit.

'Greg!' Amy dived over towards them. 'How nice to see you . . . Oh, don't eat one of those. They're horrible.' She took the dog biscuit out of his hand. 'Try one of these instead.' She grabbed for a plate of crisps and offered them to him.

Just as he was putting the crisps to his mouth, Amy saw the tell-tale dusting of chilli powder.

'Oh . . . maybe not those,' she began. 'They could be hot, they could be too spicy.'

'It's OK,' Greg said. 'I like spicy.' And he landed the handful into his mouth.

Amy watched as he chewed. He was smiling, his eyebrows waggled a little, then he swallowed and gave a little gasp.

'Phew!' he said. 'Pretty hot. But not bad.' He took a gulp of punch and then seemed to be fine.

Amy couldn't help scowling a little. This was not the plan. She'd wanted to ruin Penny's snacks, not just heat them up a little.

'Bad news!' Niffy was suddenly looming over Amy's sequinned shoulder.

'Wow, Niffy . . . is that you?' Greg teased.

'Doesn't she look gorgeous?' Min added.

'That dress is so . . .' Greg began

'Pink?' Niffy added.

'Yeah.'

'So everyone keeps telling me.'

'What's the bad news?' Amy asked.

'Four o'clock,' Niffy added.

'What?'

'Four o'clock, east by southeast . . .'

Amy's face was blank.

'Oh, for goodness sake, just look over there to the right.'

'Oh.'

'You'll see the teachers' table.'

Amy looked. '*Oh!*'

'Exactly. They've ended up with our special punch.'

A round table on the other side of the room from the

food was surrounded by eight or nine members of staff. One of the history teachers was ladling out a wineglass full of punch and handing it over to . . .

'Mrs Knebworth?' Amy whispered. 'I didn't know she was coming tonight.'

'She must have left Miss McKinnon in charge at the boarding house,' Niffy said.

'Excuse us,' Greg began, 'but we definitely have to go and dance. This is one of my favourite rhythm-and-blues numbers.'

'I can't dance to this,' Min protested.

'Just follow me,' Greg said, slipping his arm around her waist.

'Where did you put the bottle?' Amy whispered, trying not to watch Mrs Knebworth drink from her glass. But it was almost impossible not to search for any sign that the housemistress knew that the drink had been doctored.

'It's in a kitchen bin. I even wiped it for fingerprints.'

Amy snorted. 'This isn't working,' she added. 'I can't see anyone even coughing, let alone turning red and complaining about the food.'

'There you are! I've been looking for you everywhere. Where did you guys get to?' Gina asked, rushing up to them.

'You really do look good,' Amy said, distracted from the Penny sabotage project for a moment. Gina's hair was pulled back, half of it secured in a clip. Her dress was of black chiffon, pinafore style with a swishy pleated skirt and a pink silk sash; it was so understated but really pretty and totally flattering.

'Thanks. Mom always buys me a party dress as a leaving present. She can't help herself.'

'Lucky old you,' Niffy told her.

'Have you seen him, by the way?' Gina asked

'Who?' both Niffy and Amy asked together.

'Who?! My worst enemy! Charlie Fotheringham-Whatsit. He's here. I saw him come in with some of his friends.'

'Where?' Niffy asked, turning her head.

'No Angus, though,' Gina added quickly. 'But you knew he wasn't coming, right?'

'Right. He's on some charity hill walk with Finn and others from their year.'

'Girls! How fantastic to see you!' The great, posh, booming voice of Charlie Fotheringham-Whatever-it-was rolled over them. He'd grown taller. He'd dressed up for the occasion with a blue velvet jacket and a pale blue and white striped shirt which was frilly at the front: the kind of thing that only rock stars and very posh Scots could get away with.

He kissed Niffy on both cheeks, telling her with a wink how 'breathtaking' her dress was. He kissed Amy on both cheeks and took a huge handful of the crisps she offered him. He scoffed them all down and gave only the slightest of coughs before turning to Gina.

'Wow, Yankee, you look fantastic. Or should that be Yankee-doodle, you look dandy?' He roared with laughter at his own joke.

'That is just so totally feeble,' Gina said, treating him to her most withering look.

'Oh, Gina. Gina-weena, I think we need to kiss and make up. I am very sorry for all the nicknames I've given you. I am also very sorry for all the things I've done to annoy you in the past. Like punching your boyfriend and throwing cake about his café.'

'Oh, you're sorry, are you? And why would you suddenly be so sorry about all that?'

Charlie risked moving in just a little closer towards her. 'Because I've heard he's not your boyfriend any more.'

'Try these,' Amy interrupted, and offered Charlie a plate of tiny sandwiches doused in chilli powder.

He took one, ate it in one gulp and declared, 'Not bad. Not bad at all.'

'This is not working,' Amy turned to hiss at Niffy. She glanced over at Mrs Knebworth again and saw that the housemistress was holding up a dog biscuit and laughing at it. 'She knows!' Amy said, nudging Niffy in the side and getting her to look too. 'She's not about to eat that. She's laughing at it. This is not working, Nif. We have to do something much more dramatic. Oh no! Worst-case scenario!!' Amy suddenly turned to face Niffy and bent her face down to hide it. 'Jason with Penny, I can't bear it. We have to do something, Nif.'

'OK,' Niffy said, 'follow me. I have a pretty good idea.'

Chapter Thirty-five

'So it's true then about you and your waiter friend?' Charlie asked Gina.

'*Dermot,* not my waiter friend,' Gina snapped, wondering how Niffy and Amy could have been so heartless as to leave her here, stranded, with this guy. She was just going to walk away from him, she really was.

'I'm sorry. Dermot,' Charlie repeated. 'So you've broken up with him and you're not seeing anyone else at the moment?'

'Why do you want to know?'

'So I don't get into another punch-up. This is my lovely new jacket, I don't want to ruin it,' he said, smoothing down his lapels.

He somehow looked so funny doing this that Gina couldn't help smiling.

'You know, Yankee, you are very pretty when you

smile. I don't know why you're always scowling at me. I like you much, much better when you smile.'

'Well, stop bugging the hell out of me.'

'Right. I'll try . . .'

The small but incredibly enthusiastic jazz band struck up with another new number and Charlie turned to Gina with a smile. 'I know you probably want to say no . . .' he began.

'No!' Gina said.

'But you can't not dance with me.'

'No!' Gina repeated.

'There we go then, a double negative, you've just agreed.'

Before she could protest any further, he caught hold of both her hands and half pulled, half swung her onto the dance floor. He held one of her hands in his and put his arm around her waist, then he danced, leading her along in a way which was surprisingly charming and fun.

'You're quite a good dancer,' she told him, almost grudgingly.

'Ooooh, I love to dance, you should see me do my best clubbing moves.' He flung out an arm to the side to demonstrate, nearly smacking Posy in the face, and wiggled his hips.

Gina laughed.

'I feel that you and I may have got off on the wrong foot, so to speak, Yankee.'

'Are you going to stop calling me that?'

'No, it's my little nickname for you.' He pulled her in a little closer.

'If you're going to call me Yankee, then I'll call you Fatso.'

Charlie pulled a face of mock outrage. 'I'm big, but I'm not fat. See this!' He let go of her for a moment and slapped against his chest. 'Solid muscle. I'm a rugby scrum half, you know. Feel.' He pulled her hand in and slapped it against his chest.

Underneath the ruffled collar, Gina could feel firm muscle. 'Impressive,' she said.

He laughed and Gina realized that he also looked much, much better when he was smiling, not scowling.

'So how come you didn't knock Dermot down flat that time you guys were fighting?'

'Oh, I was easy on him,' Charlie said with a shrug. 'I'm quite nice, really.'

The music slowed down a little notch with the next song, but Gina realized she was not in a hurry to leave the dance floor. Charlie put both his arms around her waist and she locked her fingers round his neck . . .

Amy followed Niffy down the corridors which led in the direction of the school's main front door, the reception and both the Banshee and the deputy-headmistress's offices.

'Why are we going this way?' Amy asked. 'Do you want to land yourself with a million detentions?'

'Banshee and her mini-me are not here tonight. If they were, they'd have been in the hall. So, calm down.'

'But why are we here?'

'Well, I'm just guessing . . . but I'm hoping to find . . .' Niffy went right to the great wooden front door and began to look around the lobby. 'Do you see any cupboards? Anything like that?'

'What are we looking for, Niff?' Amy asked.

Niffy spotted a thick grey cable. 'Aha,' she said, and began to follow it through the lobby, round a corner and into a very carefully constructed low wooden cupboard, which was designed to blend in with the panelling against the wall.

'This must be it,' she said, kneeling down.

'What?' Amy asked.

Niffy didn't reply, because she had now found the small padlock which held the double cupboard doors closed.

'Hopeless,' Amy said.

'Nah. What do you want to bet that the janny uses the same code on this one that he uses on the hockey changing pavilion? Year his dog was born . . . '

Amy just watched as Niffy slid the numbers into position. *Click.* The padlock jumped open.

'Bingo!' Niffy whispered. With a quick double check over her shoulder to make sure that no one else was about, she opened the cupboard doors and revealed the school's gas meter, electricity meter and all the building's fuse boxes.

'Oh, brother!' Amy gasped.

'Yes, you *can* thank my brother; he once explained to me exactly how all this works. But all you really need to know is that this big red switch here is "off".'

'Off?' Amy repeated, getting the idea.

'Off.'

'Are we going to—?'

Before Amy could finish the question, Niffy threw the switch, and with a loud clunk the entire school plunged into darkness.

'We'd better run for it,' Niffy said, banging shut the

door and fumbling the padlock closed.

'Jeeeeeeeez!' Amy exclaimed. She grabbed hold of Niffy's dress, so bright she could just make it out as her eyes adjusted to the darkness, and followed her friend down the corridor.

Chapter Thirty-six

Creeping back into the assembly hall, Amy had to smile at the chaos.

Just enough dim light was coming in from the room's large windows to see that dancers were standing about in confusion. The staff members were on their feet, deep in frantic discussion, and Penny was rushing about the room like the proverbial headless chicken.

'Call the janitor! Where's the janitor?' she was shouting. 'Isn't he supposed to be on duty tonight? Surely he's around here somewhere! Hasn't someone gone to his office?!'

Amy spotted the silk sash first and realized she was looking at Gina's back. Arms were entwined around her. Gina was standing on her tiptoes, her head was tipped back and a tall guy was —

Gina was kissing Charlie!

Charlie!!

It had to be. That was him. That was his hair; that was his ruffled shirt. For a moment, Amy was too astonished to move, then she realized she had to rush to the rescue. She ran over to the couple and tapped Gina on the shoulder.

Gina jerked her face away from Charlie's and turned to look at her in surprise. 'Amy?'

'That's Charlie!' Amy exclaimed. 'It's dark. I don't want you to make a terrible mistake. That's Charlie.'

'She knows,' Charlie said.

'Yeah,' Gina agreed with a giggle, and the two turned to each other and began to kiss again.

'OMG,' Amy gasped to herself. She had to go and tell someone about this. Right. Now!

Niffy felt a firm hand take hold of her shoulder. A heavy hand . . . a doughy hand. A hand that had a tight hold of her.

Uh-oh. She turned and saw Mrs Knebworth standing right behind her.

'Luella?' Mrs Knebworth asked. 'I want a word with you.'

Uh-oh.

'Yes, Mrs Knebworth,' Niffy said meekly.

'Is this anything to do with you?'

'The power cut?' Niffy asked.

'Yes, Luella, the power cut.'

'Well . . .' Niffy was just about to rack her brains for a really convincing cover-up or outright denial, but then she saw that Mrs Knebworth was *smiling* at her.

'You know, I'm secretly a little bit proud of you,' Mrs Knebworth went on.

'What?!'

'Yes. Famous pranks are all part of the school legend, Luella. And you are contributing. When they write a history of the school, I hope they have a whole chapter on the most famous pranks – including the Upper Fifth dance which ended in pitch darkness.'

'Oh, this isn't nearly as good as—' Niffy stopped. She wasn't going to confess to anything else right now. Mrs Knebworth had been drinking vodka-laced punch. She might not be nearly so forgiving when she woke up in the morning.

'Now, go and switch the lights all back on again before you get into some serious trouble. There's a good girl.'

Amy had left Gina and Charlie to their quite frankly astonishing snogathon and walked around the hall, looking for someone to tell. And that was when she saw

Jason standing just a couple of metres away and looking straight at her.

Jason – oh! Still just as heart-stoppingly handsome as she remembered, maybe even more so. Dark hair, dark, dark eyes and his mouth with the soft, jutting-out lips and always a trace of a scowl about them.

Oh!

He was looking right at her and she could not breathe. What this boy, who had caused her so much upset, deserved was for her to just toss her head at him and walk on. She knew that was what she should do.

But she was rooted to the spot. She hadn't seen Jason for ages and it was just such a blood rush to see him again.

'Hey, Amy.' He spoke first. 'You look great.' He walked towards her, closing the gap. Now there was just a highly charged few centimetres or so between them. Amy was right beside him and she felt herself tingling all over. It made her think of Larson and the pool shed.

Larson had just stepped up and kissed her.

Maybe she could do that too?

'Hey, you,' she said, her voice sounding all husky.

Jason didn't say anything, but his lips parted slightly and that was enough for her to know that he was going to agree. He didn't need to say anything at all.

She moved forward and her lips brushed against his. Then she was lost in a kiss.

A totally mind-blowing I-can't-believe-it's-really-Jason kiss.

He put his arms right around her, he pulled her tightly in towards him and everything else, everyone else around them, just faded out.

She had Jason. Maybe just for a moment more, but right here and now, she had him. Already she was forgetting all about the hurtful things he had done to her in the past, and she could think only about the good times they'd had. Plus, this was Penny's boyfriend. Kissing Penny's boyfriend felt particularly good.

Bright lights seemed to dance in front of Amy's closed eyelids. *Wooooh!* This was so amazing she was seeing stars.

People were clapping!

Amy opened her eyes and saw that the hall was once again bathed in light. Bright, revealing light. Penny was standing just a couple of metres away from Jason's shoulder. She gave a scream and ran out of the assembly hall.

Now Niffy came into view, and seeing Amy's conquest and Penny's departure added, 'The charity raffle may need a new hostess. I might even offer my services.'

Amy looked up into Jason's face, saw the satisfied little sneer there, and all at once came right back to her senses. Jason was with Penny, but that hadn't stopped him for a moment. Amy could never keep him just to herself, any more than anyone else could. What he needed, more than anything else, was a taste of his own medicine.

She leaned in for one last, final, fabulous kiss. Then she broke off and stepped back.

'See ya,' she told him, then turned on her heel and walked away.

Chapter Thirty-seven

'Open another box, quick! More customers are coming,' Gina told Amy and Rosie, who were both helping her to run the charity candy stall.

The stall was on its first day, but as soon as the break bell had rung, they'd been completely inundated with customers. All the American treats which Gina had ordered online and had delivered to the school were proving hugely popular. Peanut-butter cups, Hershey bars, bubble gum in all kinds of crazy flavours, Milk Duds and Lifesavers ... everything was being snapped up as soon as they were laying it out on the table.

'What can we get you?' Amy asked Min, who had just arrived with a little gang of friends from her physics class.

'Mmmmm ... I'm just going to look for a minute. What's good? What do you recommend?'

'Are you suggesting that my assistants have been sampling the stock?' Gina said, pretending to be outraged.

'How's the cash box looking?' Amy asked.

'Bulging. I can hardly close it. And this is only day one. We're here all week! We are so going to win the one hundred pounds bonus for best idea. We've probably already made more than the fancy-dress hockey match too.'

'The novelty might wear off, though,' Min warned.

'I don't know . . .' Gina began. 'Once our customers have tasted some of this amazing stuff, they may just have to keep on coming back for more. At the end of the week, I might even let people know where they can order it for themselves.'

'You have to try these, and definitely these, and I'm sorry but there's no way I'm letting you leave without this little box here. They are complete heaven . . .' Amy insisted, giving Min and Zarah her best sales pitch.

'OK, OK. It is for a good cause, isn't it?' Zarah asked.

'UNICEF,' Gina replied. 'We decided they were best for orphans.'

'The main thing is to make loads of money,

even more money than the charity dance,' Amy added. 'As long as we make more than the dance, I will be happy.'

'You can't still need to get back at Penny?' Min asked. 'You already ruined her dance and kissed her boyfriend. Isn't that enough?'

'Well, it's not just about Penny,' Amy replied, but she looked a little guilty.

'Ooooh, talking of Penny,' Gina whispered. 'She's over there and heading this way in a hurry.'

'Uh-oh,' Min warned.

Penny's eyes were fixed on Amy; she looked a little pink with sheer fury. Gina really didn't want Penny turning up at the stall and causing a scene, so she spoke to her first. 'Hi, Penny, would you like to buy something? We have lots of great candy at special prices,' she said, trying to sound as friendly and normal as possible.

'Of course I'm not here to buy something,' Penny snapped, walking straight past Gina, her eyes still fixed on Amy.

Amy was holding onto the edge of the stall; she looked as if she was glad there was a table width between her and her furious rival.

'I am never, ever going to speak to you ever again,'

Penny snarled at Amy, her eyes flashing and her face changing from pink to a much deeper red.

Amy was beginning to blush too. But she tried to play it as casually as possible. She gave a shrug and managed to toss out a casual: 'That's fine with me. Don't think I'll be missing much.'

'And for your information, I wouldn't go out with Jason if he was the last boy on the planet.'

'Good decision, but I think you'll find you're still talking to me.'

'Never, ever again!' Penny said furiously, then she turned and marched away from the stall as quickly as she could.

'Phew!' Amy said, once Penny was safely out of earshot. 'I thought she was going to slap me or something.'

'You went way too far at the dance,' Gina told her friend.

'Ahem!' Amy cleared her throat. 'I don't think I was the only one. I mean, you were the one with your tongue down Charlie Whatsit's throat.'

The little gaggle of Lower Fourth girls who'd come along to buy sweets at the stall broke into a storm of giggling at this.

'You know, I think he might be OK,' Gina said,

realizing how pink she was turning.

'*No!*' Amy teased.

'I think I may have got him all wrong. Oh, I don't know: I kind of hate him, but I kind of like him. It's kind of hard to explain. He's a good dancer . . .'

'And kisser?' Amy wondered.

Gina just nodded and felt even more embarrassed.

'Just three more minutes to go.' Rosie checked her watch. 'Should we start packing away?'

Just then Niffy ran into the hallway where the stall had been set up.

'You're still here! Fantastic!' she exclaimed, rushing up to the counter.

'Where have you been?' Amy asked.

'Didn't have any money, had to run over to the boarding house and back to get some.'

'Niff, we'd have lent you money.'

'Nah, it's charity, I have to pay my own way. Plus, I'm intending to buy loads.' She held up the big carrier bag she was hoping to fill.

'OK!' Gina grinned. 'Let's get started.'

'Oh, and the postman's been,' Niffy added. She held up a postcard and a fat white envelope.

'For us?' Min asked.

'One for Gina,' Niffy said, handing Gina the

postcard. 'One for Aim.' She gave the fat envelope to Amy.

'Funny picture,' Niffy said, pointing at Gina's postcard. It was a trick photo of a great hairy ape cuddling a beautiful blonde girl in a bikini.

Gina was reading the back and blushing. 'It's from Charlie,' she admitted. 'He's asking me out on a date.'

'Charlie?' Niff shook her head. 'I still haven't got over that. Are you sure you didn't have a glass or two from the teachers' punchbowl?'

Gina whacked Niffy on the arm with her postcard.

'Are you going to go?' Niffy wondered.

'Of course I'm going to go. I want to know if I could be right about him . . . or if I've made the most horrible mistake.'

'Well, you definitely can't meet him at the Arts Café,' Min pointed out. 'Dermot might attack him with a muffin.'

'Death by chocolate brownie,' Niffy joked.

'What's your letter about?' Gina turned to see Amy staring at the pages in her hand with an odd expression on her face. 'Is everything OK?'

'This . . .' Amy began, her voice sounding dry. 'My dad has sent me this.'

'Yeah?' Niffy said, trying to encourage her.

'This is all the latest information on my mum. The name she's going by, her last two addresses, her parents' names and addresses and ... her phone number.'

'Oh my gosh,' Gina whispered, understanding a little of what Amy was feeling right now.

'Did you ask him to give you this?' Min wondered.

Amy nodded.

'Is she still in Glasgow?' Niffy asked.

Amy nodded again.

'What are you going to do?' Gina asked her friend.

'I don't know yet. What do you think?'

'I think it could be really ... interesting,' Gina replied.

'Yes,' Amy agreed. 'Very, very interesting.'

Niffy unwrapped a chocolate-coated peanut bar and bit down on it.

'Hey,' Min complained, 'you haven't even paid for that.'

'Don't worry, I will. Eating always helps me think. You've got to go for it, Aim,' she added through a chocolately mouthful, 'because you'll always want to know what she's really like.'

'Yes,' Amy agreed. 'I think you're right. OK ...'

'You know that we're right here to help you,' Gina added.

'Yeah . . . that's great. It really is. OK . . .' Amy took a deep breath. 'I'm going to get in touch with my mum. Finally!'

MEET THE AUTHOR . . .

CARMEN

Full name: Carmen Maria Reid

Home: A creaky Victorian house
in Glasgow, Scotland

Likes: Writing (luckily), chocolate in any shape
or form especially if caramel is involved, Jack
Russell dogs, cute blue-eyed guys in glasses,
children (especially hers), buying handbags,
holidays by the sea, Earl Grey tea in
an insulated mug, very very long walks,
very, very long jeans, shepherd's pie,
hot bubble baths (for inspiration), duvet coats,
playing tennis

Dislikes: Large animals, drinking milk (bleurrrrgh),
high heels (she's already 6ft 1), going to the gym
(but she goes anyway), filling in forms or
paperwork of any kind, flying

Would like to be: The author of lots more books
(Secret ambition was to be a ballet dancer or
Olympic gold medal winning runner)

Fascinating fact: Carmen spent four years
boarding at a girls' school very like St J's

Read about the St Jude's girls' first term together . . .

Secrets at St Jude's: New Girl
by Carmen Reid

Ohmigod! Gina's mum has finally flipped and is sending
her to Scotland to some crusty old boarding school called
St Jude's – just because Gina spent all her money on clothes
and got a few bad grades! It's so unfair!

Now the Californian mall-rat has to swap her sophisticated
life of pool parties and well-groomed boys for . . . hockey in
the rain, school dinners and stuffy housemistresses. And
what's with her three kooky dorm-buddies . . . could they ever
be her friends?

An addictive read
A hilarious read
A Carmen Reid

ISBN: 978 0 552 55706 1

Secrets at St Jude's: Jealous Girl
by Carmen Reid

Goodbye L.A., pools, malls and sunshine!

Hello Edinburgh, rain, hockey and school dinners!

Californian Gina is back in Scotland for a new term at
stuffy girls' school, St Jude's, and she's returned with
a secret jealousy.

But all the dorm girls have a reason to be jealous:
glamour-puss Amy is all green-eyed about Jason, swotty Min
longs to be like her cool friends and Niffy, stuck at home, is
jealous of everyone back at school.

The girls will have to stick together to make it
through this term!

ISBN: 978 0 552 55707 8